"DROP YOUR RIFLE!"
LONGARM CALLED.

Farrell whirled, caught sight of Longarm, and fired up at him. The slugs whined off the rockface beneath him as Longarm ducked back. When he looked over again, Farrell was scrambling back from the ledge, reaching for his horse's reins.

Pushing himself back from the edge of the rock, Longarm got to his feet and raced back down the boulder, then dropped to a narrow ledge. The rapid clink of iron on stone caused Longarm to pull up and flatten himself against a rock. Less than ten yards away, Farrell broke into the clear.

"Drop the rifle, Farrell!" Longarm shouted again.

The gambler did not have that much sense. He swung up the rifle, his eyes wild and desperate. Longarm fired up at him twice, pumping carefully each time. Farrell was hurled violently backward onto the game trail.

He did not move after he hit the ground . . .

Also in the LONGARM series
from Jove

TABOR EVANS

LONGARM

ON THE NEVADA LINE

A JOVE BOOK

LONGARM ON THE NEVADA LINE

A Jove Book/published by arrangement with
the author

PRINTING HISTORY
Jove edition/April 1985

ISBN: 0-515-08173-6

Jove books are published by The Berkley Publishing Group,
200 Madison Avenue, New York, N.Y. 10016. The words
"A JOVE BOOK" and the "J" with sunburst are trademarks
belonging to Jove Publications, Inc.

PRINTED IN THE UNITED STATES OF AMERICA

LONGARM

ON THE
NEVADA LINE

Chapter 1

Naked as a jaybird, Longarm pulled the cork out of the bottle of Maryland rye with his big, ivory-colored teeth. Tipping up the bottle, he took a hefty belt, then swished the rye around in his mouth for a moment or two before ducking his head back and gargling. Only then did he swallow the rye. So much for dental hygiene. Humming absently, he took the bottle over to the cracked china basin on a nearby stand and spiked the tepid water standing in it. Then he dipped a string washrag into the mixture and proceeded to rub himself down vigorously from hairline to shins. The cold whore-bath stung him deliciously awake.

Afterward, he strode over to his cluttered dressing table and scowled at himself in the mirror. What he saw was a lean, muscular giant on the comfortable side of forty who still had the body of a young athlete. Since coming from West-by-God-Virginia as a young man, razor-sharp winds and the searing blast of many suns had cured his rawboned features to a shade as saddle-leather brown as an Indian's. Only the gunmetal blue of his wide-set eyes and the tobacco-leaf color of his thick hair and longhorn mustache gave sure indication of his Anglo-Saxon birth—as did the hard stubble on his powerful jaw, too heavy for an Indian.

As soon as his eye caught the stubble, Longarm ran a thumbnail along the angle of his jaw.

"Sounds like you need a shave," Lenora remarked quietly from the bed, amusement in her voice.

Without turning around, Longarm nodded. "Yep. I'll have to get one on the way to the courthouse."

"See any gray hairs?"

"Nary a one," he responded, turning around to face her, a grin on his face.

Lenora Wainright was her name. She was a widow, and for the past week she had been Longarm's companion. Her home was a ranch on the high plains east of Denver—a lonely ranch, as she herself had admitted to him, since the death of her husband this past year. Longarm had met her in the lobby of the Windsor Hotel. She had been bold enough to ask him to acquaint her with the more subtle mysteries of poker, and he been more than willing to oblige. And soon they had begun the exploration of other mysteries.

At the moment Lenora was leaning back against the pillow, her crown of jet-black hair forming a darkly magnificent corona about her cleanly sculpted face. She was of Spanish ancestry, and her complexion was olive, her eyes large and lustrous. She was Longarm's age, and in her fullness as a woman. Her breasts, exposed now, were awesome in their solid amplitude, the large aureoles dark, the nipples thrusting and provocative. Beneath the white sheets he could see the outline of her hips. They were of a breadth and power capable of sending Longarm soaring, a saddle he had ridden often and long. Indeed, Lenora's passionate intensity and staying power this past week had been a revelation to Longarm. He would be sorry to see her return to her ranch. But this was her last day, and she would be taking the afternoon train.

"Are you sure you have to hurry off?" she asked.

"I told you, woman. I'm a workin' stiff."

She glanced down at him and smiled impishly. "Yes, you are that. Stiff, I mean."

He strode over to the bed and sat down beside her. Then he took her by the shoulders and kissed her on the lips, pressing himself hungrily against her. Afterward, he reached for the longjohns he had hung over the bedpost at the foot of the bed and got to his feet.

"You devil," she said, her face flushed. "You just like to drive a woman mad." She tried to turn her smile into a frown.

He shrugged. "Didn't mean no harm, ma'am," he said, pulling on his longjohns.

She watched him quietly as he pulled on his brown tweed pants. They were one size too small, and by

3

the time he had cursed the fly shut, the pants fit around his upper thighs and lean hips as snugly as a second skin.

"Why do you wear them so tight, Custis?"

"So there won't be any sweat-soaked fold of cloth between me and the saddle when I ride." He hauled on a pair of woolen socks, then reached for his boots, low-heeled cavalry stovepipes.

"Are you planning on riding far today?"

"Met Wallace in the lobby yesterday. He said Billy Vail had an assignment for me. Knowing Billy, it'll be a long way from here."

"And from me."

His boots on, he sat back down on the bed beside her.

"I thought we weren't going to talk about that any more," he told her gently. "You're going back to your ranch, and I'm going back to work."

"I know. Forgive me." Then she looked into his eyes searchingly. "Custis, hasn't it been nice? I mean, between us."

"Sure has," he grinned, placing his big hand over hers and squeezing. "It's been better than that."

"Then . . . why not come back with me? To the ranch, I mean. Run it for me—with me. Then later, maybe . . ."

He saw where she was heading. In fact, he had been half expecting her to come up with such a proposal for the past couple of days. Off and on, she had been hinting at such an arrangement. For his part, he had been preparing himself mentally, hoping he would have the right words to explain to her why it was a

4

possibility he could not accept.

As gently as he could, he said, "Lenora, ranching just ain't my style. Not now, anyway. As long as I can, I want to be able to ride out anywhere Billy sends me. Or anywhere I send myself, if it comes to that. What keeps me going, I guess, is not knowing what's waiting for me on the other side of the mountain."

"Just another mountain, Custis."

"Maybe—maybe not. You can't be sure. And I guess that's what keeps me going."

"Have you thought what a challenge this ranch could be, Custis? And you'd make it hum. A man like you."

"Sure. And at first I'd like it fine. But before long the days would be coming at me pretty fast, one after the other, a steady stream, like telegraph poles—each one pretty much like the one before. And the next time I looked up, I'd be old and wondering where the years had gone, and all I'd have to show for those years would be more cattle, maybe, and a larger house."

"And a woman who loved you. And a pride of children. Young lions you had sired."

Longarm shrugged. "Sure. That would be nice, Lenora. I ain't saying it wouldn't. And it's something a man has to think about. But I've seen the price some men've paid for that. I guess right now it's a price I am not yet willing to pay."

"Well, then," she said, smiling bravely, a single tear coursing down one cheek, "I guess that settles it."

He closed both hands around hers. "You ain't hurting, are you, Lenora? Hell, we don't have to be

5

strangers. Denver ain't that far. And I'll be out to visit whenever I can."

She shook her head sadly. "No, Custis. There's a rancher nearby. He's been widowed for a couple of years now, and he's already suggested we join forces. I came to Denver to get some thinking done, and to maybe kick up my heels one last time."

He grinned suddenly at her. "Well, now, you sure as hell did that."

"Yes. And I'll never be sorry. Never. But it is time now for me to get on with a more . . . sensible style of living."

"This rancher . . . you like him?"

"Yes. I respect him and I like him. He was a good friend of my husband's. I have known him for years. He does not excite me. But I am sure we will make a good . . . partnership."

"I hope you will be very happy, Lenora."

She tipped her head. "Happy, Custis? Why is it that everyone talks about being happy all the time? Happiness has nothing at all to do with life. Not with life as it must be lived."

Longarm sat back. He was aware suddenly of a dimension in Lenora he had not suspected. "I reckon that's true." He smiled. "Damn, but you sure are philosophical this morning."

She smiled, and this time it was she who reached out to take Longarm's hand. "I didn't mean to put you off, Custis. Just wish me luck. No one can have too much of that."

He leaned forward and kissed her full lips, drinking in their wondrous warmth, and for a moment he found himself wondering if he wasn't making the biggest mistake of his life.

"All right," he said, sitting back, then getting to his feet. "I wish you luck. All the luck you need."

She smiled bravely up at him. "And I wish you luck also, Custis."

She leaned back against the pillow and drew the sheet up around her, a modest blush on her face for the first time since he had known her.

Feeling strangely at odds with himself, Longarm finished dressing, aware of Lenora's quiet eyes watching him. As he tucked a clean linen handkerchief into the breast pocket of his brown frock coat finally and reached for his snuff-brown Stetson, he glanced down at her.

"So I guess this is goodbye, Lenora."

"I know."

He leaned over and kissed her lightly on her cheek. He tasted a trace of salt. Straightening, he clapped on the hat, tilting it slightly forward, cavalry-style, and walked to the door.

"I'll leave later," she told him, "after a decent interval."

"It's been a whole lot better than nice, Lenora," he told her, pulling open the door.

"Thank you, Custis. For me, too."

He stepped out of the room and pulled the door shut behind him. For a moment he stood in the hallway, feeling strangely empty. The weight of the double-action .44-40 Colt in the cross-draw rig under his frock coat felt suddenly heavy—oppressively so. Then, with a determined stride, he started quickly down the hallway, wondering what Billy Vail had for him.

He hoped it was just as far from Denver as Wallace had hinted it might be.

In his salad days Marshal Billy Vail had mixed it up with Comanche, owlhoots, and more than likely half of Mexico. He was carrying too much lard now and wearing that weary look that came from sitting too long in one place. It was a look Longarm associated with the courthouse gang, as he called them.

At the moment Billy Vail was pawing through the papers on his desk for the folder he was looking for. At last, with a deep sigh, he hauled it out from under the clutter and opened it, one bushy eyebrow cocked.

"You ever hear of a gent named Warner?" Vail asked.

"Babe Warner?"

"That's the son of a bitch. We been looking for him for too damn long now for a series of train robberies he masterminded in California. The Pinkertons have been looking, too. But I'd sure like to nail this bastard before the Pinkertons get wind of his whereabouts."

"Any chance of that?"

"Not unless they get hold of the gent we got sitting downstairs in the jug. His name's Pete Bowdoin. He was part of Warner's gang, and he just made a deal with me. He told me where Warner's holed up if I promised to speak to the judge for him and maybe get him a lighter sentence."

"So where *is* Warner?"

8

"A cowtown upriver from Miles City on the Yellowstone. Snake Flat, it's called. The place is a haven for gunslicks on the run and those with dirty money hankering to find land. According to Bowdoin, Warner's callin' himself Jake Telford. He's struttin' around pretty handsome, making noises like a big cattleman."

"Maybe he's gone straight."

"Straight, hell! The statute of limitations ain't run out yet, Longarm, and he's still on our Wanted list."

Longarm took out a cheroot and lit it. "So you want him."

"I want him. The only thing is, Telford might be Warner, or he might not be. You know I can't really trust Bowdoin. And I've never had a description of Babe Warner to go on. No one has. So we can't match this fellow Telford up with a physical description. Outside of Bowdoin's testimony, there's no solid way to verify that Telford is Babe Warner."

Longarm rested his cheroot in the ashtray on the corner of Vail's desk and took the folder. "How long we been looking for Warner?"

"Eight years."

Longarm glanced through the folder. The infamous Babe Warner had been a most efficient train robber, judging from the amounts he had taken. But, as Billy Vail had just testified, the folder contained little or no physical description.

Longarm gave the folder back to Vail and picked his cheroot up off the desk. "You're right, chief. There's damn little here for me to go on. But even so, there's no telling what a man would look like after eight years, anyway."

Billy Vail nodded. "My thoughts exactly."

"So what do you suggest?"

"Go there and sniff around, Longarm. Get to know this Telford. Join up with him if you can. You should be able to do that without much trouble, I figure. You're part outlaw yourself."

"Thanks for them kind words, Billy. And after I've joined his gang of gunslicks, you figure this rancher Telford might loosen up and spill his ugly past to me."

Vail shrugged. "I don't figure anything for sure, Longarm. You know that. Life ain't nearly that simple. Just play the cards you get dealt and keep your ass covered like you usually do. If this here Telford's got a ranch, like Bowdoin says, maybe you might do a little hard work for a change, punchin' cattle."

"This is getting to sound better every minute," Longarm drawled, smiling at Vail.

"Just make sure you keep your badge hid. I got a feeling that place up there might turn into a real mean place for you once the citizens cotton to who you are."

Longarm nodded. "Maybe I better do more than keep my badge hid," he acknowledged. "There's more than a few gunslicks west of the Mississippi know me—and this little surprise I carry with me." Longarm patted the double-barrelled .44 derringer resting in his vest pocket. "I'll keep the derringer in my right boot and carry my .44 in a side holster."

Vail nodded. "That sounds like a very good idea."

Longarm put out his cheroot in the ashtray and stood up. Clapping his hat on, he looked somberly down at the chief. "Maybe you don't know how glad I am to get out of this mile-high Sodom and Gomorrah, chief. I think maybe I been town-pent too long."

Vail leaned back in his seat, his eyes revealing a sudden concern. "Glad to hear that, Longarm. I was beginning to wonder about you and that widow and that fine ranch of hers east of here. I don't mind tellin' you. I was startin' to hear talk. You and her been pretty thick."

"I'm not ready for the harness yet, chief. But she's some woman. I could have done a whole lot worse."

"I know that, Longarm."

Longarm started for the door. "Do you think that little boy secretary of yours could have my travel vouchers ready by the time I get back with my gear?"

"I'll see to it."

"Thanks."

As Longarm opened the door, Vail got to his feet. "Just be damned sure you make it back here in one piece, Longarm. With or without Babe Warner."

"I'll do what I can," Longarm said, pulling the door shut behind him.

Longarm got his first glimpse of the woman as the stage neared the way station a few miles north of the Yellowstone, the last stop before Snake Flat. At first the woman was but a splash of brightness against the square stone building. Before long, however, he could see her quite clearly.

She was tall and had braced her back against the wall of the way station. She was wearing a long navy blue cloak, which the constant wind molded against her full body. She should have been wearing a bonnet or a traveling hat of some kind. Instead, she wore her

11

thick, reddish hair loose, allowing it to flow luxuriantly down over her shoulders. Occasionally a gust of wind lifted a thick curl against her face. As the stagecoach rattled into the way station, she turned to watch it, revealing the single large trunk—an ancient portmanteau—that had been hidden beside her.

Longarm was the stage's sole passenger. The jehu had offered to let him ride up beside him on the box, but Longarm had declined the offer. Now he pushed open the narrow coach door and climbed out, grateful for the chance to stretch his legs. He was no longer wearing his snuff-brown Stetson. In its place he wore a black, flat-crowned plainsman's hat. The rest of his uniform had changed just as radically. Instead of his customary brown tweed pants, frock coat, and vest he was wearing a heavy fringed buckskin shirt and Levi's. His Colt he carried in a greased, flapless holster strapped to his thigh, and the derringer was strapped to the back of his leg in a small leather pocket just above the top of his boot.

The driver had told Longarm he was hoping to pick up passengers as well as a change of horses at this station, for here the north-south road crossed with the looping ruts that followed Yellowstone upriver from Miles City. Apparently, the tall woman in the navy blue cloak was one of the new passengers. As Longarm neared the woman on his way to the station, he touched the brim of his hat to her.

She frowned. "The stage is late," she said. "At least an hour."

"At least," Longarm agreed, pulling up and facing

her. "But if it had been me driving over those roads, I don't think we would have made it at all."

She looked beyond Longarm to the dust-laden stage. "I must admit I am not looking forward to climbing back into a stage." She smiled at him then. "Would you be so kind as to help me with my trunk?"

She seemed quite used to approaching strangers in out-of-the-way places and making use of them, he noticed.

"Of course."

As he hefted the trunk onto his shoulders, the jehu brushed past him on his way to the way station, muttering something about this being a chance to eat. The stock tender was busy changing the horses. As Longarm walked toward the stage, his vision blocked by the trunk, he could hear the slap of leather and the stamping of the fresh horses as they were backed into the traces. Reaching the coach, Longarm deposited the trunk into the rear boot and looked back at the woman.

"Is this all your luggage?"

"I have one more small piece in the way station," she told him. "I'll get it."

When she reappeared with the suitcase, he took it from her and stored it beside the portmanteau, then accompanied her inside the way station. She sat down at a table apart from the driver and a third passenger.

Longarm excused himself to wash up at the pump outside and returned in time to see what was being placed down before the stage driver: bread and bacon, washed down with strong tea without sugar or milk, a concoction called slumgullion. From experience, Longarm knew that it tasted even worse than it sounded. He decided against dining.

Sitting back down at the table beside the woman, he glanced at the third passenger, a slender man in his late twenties, dressed in black, with a thin wisp of a mustache. His long face was sensitive, his fingers graceful and tapering. They were the hands of a gambler. Looking idly away from the man, Longarm looked back at the woman.

"My name is Rose," she told him at once, without him having to ask. "Rose Gantry. I am on my way to Snake Flat. I am a singer."

"Custis Long," he told her. "I'm heading for the same place. I don't sing. Maybe I'll find me something to do in Snake Flat. Maybe I won't."

She nodded, her eyes boldly taking in his deerskin shirt and the gleaming Colt in its holster. It was clear she regarded him as a drifter. This did not bother Longarm in the slightest, since this was precisely the impression he was hoping to give to her and anyone else he met.

He returned her frank appraisal. She was handsome rather than pretty, her cheekbones prominent, her chin bold and uncompromising. Her mouth was wide and expressive and her lips were full. From under long lashes, her steel-gray eyes watched him with a wary interest. It was obvious from her unswerving gaze that she was used to dealing with men—and more than a match for most.

Abruptly, the dingy dimness of the place made him

restless. He excused himself, got up, and went outside. Rose Gantry made no effort to accompany him and indeed seemed relieved that he was not about to impose his presence on her any longer than his kindness to her warranted. He had already served his purpose, as far as she was concerned, when he had deposited her luggage in the coach's rear boot—something that neither the gambler or the stove-up jehu could have managed as easily.

Ten minutes later they were ready to leave. The driver left the station, climbed to his perch, and inclined his head to Longarm. But again Longarm declined the honor and stepped into the coach. Rose Gantry and the gambler took the rear seat, and though there was room for three on it, Longarm took the forward seat and sat facing them. The jehu's whip cracked, he let out a damning string of curses at his team, and the coach lurched forward. In a moment, they were rocking out of the way station.

They made a silent threesome inside the coach. The woman sat with her hands calmly folded in her lap. Her gaze, when it touched Longarm, held neither animosity nor interest. Longarm realized that she had already dismissed him as a drifter, and let it go at that. The gambler beside her was content to stare out at the landscape, his pale face troubled, his eyes bleak. So far, Longarm realized, he had not heard the man utter a word.

The swaying of the coach on its leather thoroughbraces gave a rocking, hammock-like effect that soon lulled all three of them. The late-afternoon sun hammered upon the coach. Dust found its way in through the open windows. From time to time the woman coughed.

The landscape was undergoing a change. After the hills of Wyoming, there had been rolling plains until they reached the breaks of the Yellowstone, a land studded by sage and wild rose and blue lupine, with pine and stout juniper showing on the rimrocks that followed the road. Now the country ran flatter, and one could see so long into the distance that his thoughts took to flight, as if in seeing that far a man could see into his own past—or, worse, into his future. An unaccountable ache fell over Longarm and he found himself thinking of that single, solitary tear rolling down Lenora Wainright's face.

As soon as the road began to climb, he shook off his melancholy. Timber showed more frequently, and the far horizons were gone. Huge rock piles littered this land, giant heaps of sandstone molded by wind and rain into weird shapes. Wild currant and gooseberry showed, and forget-me-nots on tall stalks waved in the wind as the coach clattered on past.

The deeper they drove into this country, the thicker the timber became, and the higher, more ponderous and threatening became the great heaps of rocks. The road wound closer now to dangerous ravines and canyons. At times, glancing out the side window, all Longarm could see was the distant tops of pines crawling slowly along beneath the coach. Longarm wondered why a lighter mud wagon, built closer to the ground than this Concord coach, was not used on this run.

The afternoon was more than half gone when the stage toiled to the top of a rise and the jehu pulled it to a stop in the shadow of a cliffside.

"Time to give the horses a chance to blow," the old man proclaimed, clambering down from his perch and yanking open the coach door. "Anybody want a drink, there's a creek yonder." He pointed down a slope.

Longarm climbed out, grateful for the solid feel of the earth beneath his feet. Free now of the coach's stifling enclosure, he could hear plainly the cool music of the running water below him. He turned to the woman, offering with an inclination of his head to escort her to the stream. She shook her head.

Longarm left the trail, skirted two massive rocks sitting by the roadside, and started down through the fragrant pines, his feet feeling like stumps. But he moved swiftly, easily through the brush and then down through the aisles of trees toward the stream bank. It was a good hundred yards from the road, and he felt the pull of exertion on his ankles and the needle-like crawl of perspiration on his back before he reached the stream.

Removing his hat, he lowered himself onto the stones bordering the stream and ducked his entire head under the swift, icy water. The shock was more than invigorating; it was life-giving. Lifting his head back out of the water, he shook his hair to dry it and repeatedly ran his big hands through the thick, luxuriant coils. Then he lowered his mouth to the water and drank deep, like the wild animal he had nearly become at that moment.

Standing, he looked about him for a moment, dimly aware of the whisper of the water as it fled over the rocks. In this isolation of brush and stream and sky, he felt almost reborn. His overlong lay-up in Denver had had the effect of blunting this awareness of the real world of sun and sky, brush and timber, the mint-like flavor of it. He had become used to the smoke-filled saloons, the all-night poker games, the littered streets, and the coal smoke pumping into the sky of the crowded, unfeeling, stinking metropolis. For a while back there, he had almost come to think of Denver and the ranches and hills surrounding it as the world.

And for Lenora Wainright that was what it was. But not for him. Never. In that instant his melancholy lifted from him. No longer was he wondering if he had made the correct decision. He knew for certain now that he had.

He turned away from the creek and started up the slope to the roadway. As he worked his way through the timber, he moved as silently as a large cat. He was only a few yards below the roadway when he came to a sudden, wary halt, all his senses alert. The wind had brought him a discordant sound, and now he listened as an ugly voice, its tone sharp and commanding, came from the direction of the stage. The voice did not belong to the driver, and Longarm had difficulty believing it could be coming from that silent, morose gambler beside the woman. Again the voice came, cold and rasping, as unpleasant as fingernails dragged across a blackboard.

18

Directly above him was one of the many boulders that lined the roadway. Drawing his .44 from his holster, Longarm vaulted up the steep face of it, traveled about a dozen feet, then found himself at its pinnacle. Peering carefully over the top, he saw the coach below and, backed against it, his two fellow passengers and the jehu.

The driver's ancient face was livid with anger as he kept both hands over his head. The woman, Rose, stood without flinching, her eyes fixed coldly on the highwayman approaching her. The gambler stood beside her, his lidded eyes watching angrily. There were three highwaymen in all. Two were mounted, their guns leveled on the passengers, while the third was approaching the passengers on foot. All three outlaws had yanked bandannas up over their faces and had pulled their hat brims down over their foreheads as well, so that only their predatory eyes were visible.

The one approaching Rose said something nasty and reached out for a chain he had spied around the woman's neck. She stepped back and slapped the outlaw, the stinging sound of it carrying all the way to Longarm.

"I'll hand it to you!" she told the highwayman. "Keep your dirty paws off me."

The highwayman had rocked back in surprise and indignation. The two mounted outlaws immediately burst into laughter at his discomfiture. Furious, the highwayman moved in and yanked the necklace from around the woman's neck. When she cried out and tried to grab it back, he punched her brutally in the stomach. The woman gasped and folded over. Only the gambler's quick hands kept her from pitching forward onto the ground.

"Let her go," the highwayman told the gambler, "and give me your wallet."

"No," the gambler said.

One of the horsemen pulled out his gun and cocked it. Aiming it carefully at the gambler, he spoke sharply. It was the same voice Longarm had heard from the slope. "Let go of that woman and hand over your wallet or I'll drop you where you stand."

Longarm aimed and fired. The gun went flying from the outlaw's hand. The outlaw on the ground spun, clawing for his own weapon. Longarm swung his Colt and fired, catching the man belt-high. As he clasped his belly and plunged forward into the dust, the other two riders wheeled their horses and galloped off.

Longarm sent one more round after them before clambering down from the rock. The downed outlaw's hands were frantically clutching his stomach in a futile effort to staunch the livid flow. Undiminished, the black blood poured through his dirty, splayed fingers. As the man writhed in his death agony, the bandanna slipped down off his face.

"Damn!" cried the jehu. "That's Hank Dennim. Them other two must've been his brothers."

Longarm went down on one knee beside Dennim. But the outlaw did not see Longarm. He was staring instead into the awful, devouring eyes of death. After a moment, the light in the outlaw's eyes faded. His hands dropped away from the hole in his gut. Holstering his Colt, Longarm took from the dying man's grasp the necklace and brooch Dennim had but a moment before wrenched brutally from Rose Gantry's neck.

"I'll take that," the gambler said.

Longarm handed it up to him. The gambler took it and handed it to Rose. Clasping it quickly, she dropped it quickly into her bosom, then turned away, her face drawn, her eyes stark.

Longarm looked back down at the outlaw. He was dead. Longarm stood up. The gambler's eyes were fixed coolly on Longarm.

"What now, stranger?" he asked.

"I'll need some help getting him off the road."

The gambler nodded. The two men reached down, each one taking a hand. Dragging the dead outlaw to the edge of the road, they pitched him off into the pines. Walking back to the stagecoach, Longarm suggested to the jehu that he could see to it that someone was sent back after the outlaw's body when they reached Snake Flat.

"Hell," the driver sniffed, "they ain't no one gonna bother about that no-account. Let him feed the buzzards. That'd be the best use he's ever been, to my way of thinking."

Longarm shrugged.

The stunned Rose was looking at Longarm now with something approaching awe in her eyes. Her earlier appraisal, that he was not much more than a drifter, had altered drastically, it seemed.

21

"Let's get this stage movin'!" the jehu cried, turning away and clambering up onto the box. "We got a ways to go yet before we reach Snake Flat!"

The gambler opened the stage door for Rose. She turned about and stepped up into the coach, the gambler following. Longarm climbed in after them. Pulling the door shut, he sat down facing the two. The jehu's whip cracked and the stage lurched forward.

Rose, her face as pale as an old newspaper, cleared her throat and moistened her dry lips. Her voice was somewhat shaky as she said to Longarm, "I have never seen death that close. It . . . it was not pleasant."

"No, it wasn't," Longarm agreed.

"I suppose I must thank you for retrieving this brooch. And I do. It was a gift from my mother."

"You don't owe me a thing, Rose," Longarm replied.

She nodded, then looked away. It was too unsettling, it seemed, for her to look any longer into the eyes of a man who had just cut short the life of a fellow human, no matter how despicable that dead man might have been.

"You handle your gun like an expert, mister," the gambler commented.

Longarm caught the cold contempt in the gambler's words. His remark was not meant as a compliment.

"The name's Long," Longarm told him. "Custis Long."

The gambler smiled thinly and dutifully held out his slender hand. "Farrell," he said as Longarm and he shook hands. "Lucky Farrell."

"Are you?"

"Lucky?" The gambler smiled sardonically. "I guess I am at that." He tapped his breast pocket. "I'm carrying a sizable amount of paper currency in this billfold."

Longarm looked back at Rose. The color had begun to return to her face, but she could still not bring herself to look into his eyes. Longarm was suddenly weary. Only now was he beginning to feel the tension aroused by the brief, deadly gun battle. He felt suddenly drained. Closing his eyes, he leaned his head back against the leather cushion.

Before long the swaying of the coach lulled him and he dozed.

himself a washing, using up most of the water in the pitcher. Shaving next in the cold dregs of water that remained, he shrugged into a fresh buckskin shirt, clapped his hat back on, and went downstairs to the hotel dining room.

He was as empty as a rain barrel in August and with quiet, bitter relish ate a solitary meal. After that interminable stagecoach ride and the violent death that had abruptly punctuated its last miles, Longarm was grateful to find himself apart from Rose Gantry and Farrell. There were times, and this was one of them, when he craved solitude the way a thirsty man craves water. He needed time to digest and accept the necessity for the violence he had so recently experienced.

This afternoon was not the first time Longarm had killed a man, and it would not be the last. The highwayman had been about to kill him. Longarm had had no alternative but to do what he had. Still, he could not help recalling the look in Rose Gantry's eyes, or the cold, appraising gaze of the gambler. Though Longarm did not see himself as they did, it was not all that easy to discount the accusation he sometimes read in the face of others, no matter how naive and simplistic their harsh judgment might be.

He paid up and left the hotel. It was dusk. Around him, Snake Flat's night life swirled. He could hear the clatter of the saloons and the constant rumble of men's voices. As he tramped along the boardwalk, he found himself elbowing his way through a steady, pressing tide of unkempt, gun-heavy men. He saw that the blacksmith shop was now closed, as was a general store he passed. He was trying to get a feel for the place, convinced there would be a time when he might need the knowledge.

Horses crowded the hitch racks, and he memorized their brands without conscious volition. He saw a number of bearded, booted railroad workers and roustabouts and remembered the jehu mentioning that a railroad spur was pushing its way south and was already eating its way through the hills less than twenty miles from Snake Flat. When it crossed this valley, Longarm reflected, it would bring a hectic, burgeoning prosperity.

He passed a print shop and a millinery and a saddle shop, all dark at this hour. A single lamp glowed deep within the recesses of a livery stable. Beyond this was Snake Flat's only brick building—the bank. It was called the Snake Valley Cattleman's Savings and Loan. Longarm glanced at the gold lettering on its window and pulled up, startled.

Jake Telford's name was listed as president.

He read it over twice. Telford was obviously a big man in these parts. Shaking his head in surprise, Longarm kept on past the bank until he came to the largest and most luxurious saloon in the town, the Bagdad. He mounted the porch and shouldered his way through the batwings. He stood in the doorway for a moment, looking the place over. Then he walked over to the bar, impressed by the saloon's elegance. He had not expected this in Snake Flat. The more Longarm thought about it, the more he marveled at the opulent exile Babe Warner and his fellow outcasts seemed to have found for themselves.

The mahogany bar was long, with a mirror behind it. In the back there were at least a score of gaming tables. A small stage filled one end of the room. Smoke lay in blue layers and a piano tinkled incessantly. At least fifty men were crowded into the place: punchers from the valley ranches, construction workers from the railroad, and citizens of the town.

Longarm ordered whiskey and took the bottle with him over to a small table along the far wall, passing a blackjack table on the way. Sitting with his back to it, he continued to look over the place. There was an upstairs balcony running around three sides of the main barroom. Longarm caught a glimpse of the gay skirt of a percentage girl on the runway above and heard a door slam. He smiled. Here was a well-stocked saloon providing all the pleasures.

The whiskey warmed him. As he listened to the pleasant rumble of talk all around him, he felt some of the tension draining out of him. Glancing up, he saw a percentage girl approaching his table. There was a bold, inviting smile on her face. He shook his head, not unkindly, and filled his glass.

She came to a halt and stood uncertainly in front of his table.

"What is it?" he asked.

"I was supposed to keep you company," she said. "But don't worry. You don't have to pay."

"If I don't, who does?"

"That gentleman over there," she said, indicating a heavily bearded fellow, who had glanced up from his poker game and was watching Longarm. As soon

28

as he caught Longarm's eye, the fellow smiled and nodded a greeting.

Longarm did not think he knew the man, but for just an instant there seemed to be something vaguely familiar about him. Frowning, Longarm nodded back. The bearded fellow went back to his poker game, his face wreathed in cigar smoke.

"Who's the gentleman?" Longarm asked.

"That's Mike. He said to tell you he was just an admirer. I guess he heard about the way you handled that Dennim gang this afternoon."

"What do you know about it?" he inquired, curious.

She brightened. "Oh, I heard all about it. Everyone in town has."

"I see." He smiled up at her. "What's your name?"

"Marie."

"Well, Marie, it's nothing personal, but I think I've had about all the excitement I can handle for one day. Some other time, maybe. And give the gentleman my thanks."

She seemed a little disappointed, but nodded courteously and moved off through the packed saloon. He watched her pick her way around the tables. As she stopped to say something to the bearded poker player, she was grabbed eagerly by a huge, not too clean cowpuncher who had just barged into the saloon.

Longarm looked away and sipped his drink.

Abruptly, the curtain on the little stage jerked open. The piano player beat out a fanfare of sorts, and Longarm saw Rose Gantry step out onto the low platform. She wore a long russet gown that clung to her tightly,

29

enhancing the voluptuous fullness of her statuesque figure. The gown was cut to leave her shoulders and forearms bare and allowed a glimpse of the shadowy cleft formed by her full breasts. Her rich, auburn hair was piled high, an ornate comb holding it. Her earrings were of elegant jade.

Longarm was impressed, as were the rest of the saloon's patrons. The place hushed almost instantly.

Rose took another small step forward, her face suddenly aglow in the light from the sputtering kerosene footlights. She smiled, clasped her hands before her, and began to sing in a low, throaty voice.

Everyone in the place listened as if smitten into silence. The song she sang was an old one, known to all, a sentimental ballad that spoke of loneliness and of girls left behind. She sang it with a voice that caressed the unruly crowd, taming it completely. When she finished, she curtsied quickly and bowed, then stepped back.

The curtain jerked closed and the place broke into a storm of applause. A spangle-skirted bar girl appeared on the stage, kicking high, and the piano went wild. The patrons went back to their former occupations, but above the sound of clicking dice and rattling chips, Longarm heard the steady murmur of surprise and pleasure aroused by Rose Gantry's singing.

Longarm started to leave and saw Lucky Farrell get up from a poker table in the company of a stocky, prosperous-looking merchant and head directly for his table. Relaxing back into his chair, Longarm waited for the two men to reach his table.

"Mr. Long," Farrell said, "this here is Ogden Maxwell. When he found out you and I were fellow passengers on the stage this afternoon, he asked if I might introduce you."

"It's a pleasure, Mr. Long," Maxwell said heartily, reaching out a pudgy hand.

Longarm took it and pumped it once. The man's handshake was slightly damp and not very powerful. He was dressed in a gray frock coat and vest, the latter stretched tightly over his ample bay window. On his balding head sat a gray fedora. His narrow, fashionable shoes were resplendent in gleaming white spats.

"Sit down," Longarm said, "and join me in a drink."

"Why, that's most kind of you," Maxwell said, pulling a chair over and slumping heavily into it. "I see you favor my brand."

"Yes," Longarm said, waving over a bar girl.

When she arrived, Longarm asked for another glass. As she hastened back toward the bar, Farrell said, "Guess I'll be getting back to my game, gents." Nodding goodbye to Maxwell and Longarm, the gambler turned and threaded his way back to his table.

Maxwell's glass arrived. Longarm filled it. Maxwell threw down the whiskey as if it were water. His face was round and flabby, its color shrimp pink. Small exploded veins stood out on his nose and his green eyes shone like buttons as he regarded Longarm.

"What can I do for you, Mr. Maxwell?" Longarm inquired.

"Call me Max," the man said. "Everyone in town does."

Longarm nodded and leaned back in his chair to

wait for Maxwell to explain his reason for wanting to meet with him. He did not invite Maxwell to address him as Custis.

Clearing his throat, Maxwell began. "The whole town knows, Mr. Long, how you handled Hank Dennim this afternoon."

Longarm inclined his head slightly in acknowledgment.

"I am the president of Snake Flat's town council," Maxwell continued, "and I think you are just what this town—this entire valley, in fact—needs. A strong hand and quick gun to clear out the gunslicks and other undesirables who have been flooding this town for the past five years and longer."

"And just how do you suggest I go about accomplishing that feat?"

"We will appoint you town marshal. But that's only for starters. Later, we will back you for the position of county sheriff."

"Don't you already have a town marshal?"

"We do. His name is Lester Boggs. He wouldn't make half of you, and he ain't worth a pitcher of warm spit."

"I don't know, Max. Seems to me you're jumpin' the gun. What do you know about me?"

"What are you implying, sir?"

"Maybe I'm just one more gunslick—another outcast looking for a place to hide."

Maxwell leaned back in his chair and regarded Longarm shrewdly. "Mr. Long," he said, "that may be true. And, to be perfectly honest, I don't really care. The fact is, you've taken on the Dennims. That means there's no way short of killing the whole passel of them that you'll find any real sanctuary here, apart from a badge and my support."

"That so?"

"Unfortunately, yes, Mr. Long. Some flannel-mouths around here talk a big show, but they're all gurgle and no guts. The Dennims are a different kettle of fish. When they ride into Snake Flat, hell takes a holiday. And it ain't just Bo and Will I'm thinkin' of now. It's their pa, Silas. He's a big man and a mean one."

Longarm smiled. "They sure don't sound very sociable, at that."

Maxwell's face grew even redder as he thought about the Dennims. "They are as sociable as an ulcerated tooth. It's families like the Dennims that are holdin' back the development of this here valley, Mr. Long. That's why I'm hoping you'll throw in with those of us who, like you, are willing to stand up to them."

"You mean you'd like me to help you drive the Dennims out of here?"

"You put things bluntly, Mr. Long. But the answer is just as blunt. Yes."

"Anyone else in particular, Max?"

Maxwell hesitated only a moment. "Jake Telford."

Longarm reached for his glass. "You mean he's worse than the Dennims? What's he done?"

"The Dennims represent—at worst—a manageable nuisance. Telford is a far more serious threat."

"How so?"

"Jake Telford has bought up some of the best ranches

in this valley. But he's not satisfied. He wants the entire valley."

"He's got a big appetite, has he?"

"Yes," snapped Maxwell. "In the last eight years he's been driving cattlemen from this valley, then buying up their ranges cheap. Now he's gone ahead and formed a syndicate with himself and his fellow outcasts at the head. Unless he can be stopped, Jake Telford will be the only rancher left shipping cattle from this valley."

"Didn't I see Telford's name on that bank outside?"

"Yes. Fortunately, it is not the only bank in town. Even so, with those resources at his disposal, Jake Telford is tightening his ruthless hands about the necks of every honest merchant and cattleman in the valley."

Longarm leaned back and regarded the fat man shrewdly. "Looks like you've got two mighty unhappy war parties in Snake Flat—and each one getting ready to have a go at the other."

"I'm afraid that is true."

"And you figure I should choose one of the two war parties."

"If you intend to remain here for any length of time."

"Then maybe I'd be doing myself a whole lot better if I joined up with Telford. He looks pretty big from where I'm sitting."

A thin, ironic smile creased Maxwell's face. "That might indeed be your wisest course—if it were not for the Dennims."

"They ride with Telford?"

"They do indeed. Telford and the Dennims arrived

34

in this valley together many years ago. They are hogs who grunt at the same trough. Scratch one and you'll find the other."

"I see," Longarm said, pursing his lips thoughtfully as he sipped his drink.

"Well, Mr. Long, can we count on you?"

Longarm finished his whiskey and slapped the glass down on the table. "Thanks. But no thanks," he told Maxwell. "I don't see myself as a lawman. At least not in this town. It wouldn't be all that healthy."

"The town council would back you to the hilt."

"Ain't this here Telford on the council?"

"Yes, but he has only two votes—himself and his stooge."

Longarm chuckled. "Only two, huh? Well, I got a feeling that vote of his is going to grow some."

Maxwell sat back suddenly in his chair, his eyes no longer so friendly. "Then you won't throw in with us?"

"That's right."

"And this is your final word?"

Longarm nodded.

"I think it would be in your best interests to reconsider."

Longarm did not like the sound of that. It was a threat the man had not even bothered to veil. Longarm became suddenly very weary of Maxwell. Without bothering to answer the man, Longarm took out a cheroot and lit up. He was not careful where he blew the smoke.

Maxwell's smiling affability vanished. Downing his drink, he shoved himself to his feet and, with a curt nod, turned and stalked from the saloon.

As Longarm watched him go, he became aware of a slight, rising murmur that spread to every corner of the place. From the moment Lucky Farrell had brought Maxwell over to his table, Longarm realized, the subsequent parley had been watched closely by almost everyone in the place.

The pianist suddenly beat out his fanfare and Rose Gantry appeared again on the small stage. Clasping her hands as before, she sang her last song of the evening. Once again her dark, lovely voice quieted the saloon magically, and when she had finished the saloon's patrons were aroused to an even greater storm of applause than before.

It appeared that Rose Gantry was becoming quite a hit in Snake Flat.

Longarm took his bottle by its neck and left the saloon.

Once he reached his room, Longarm took the usual precautions before turning in. Crumpling up wads of newspaper he had brought up with him from the hotel lobby, he scattered them about the floor. Then he turned off the lamp on the bedside table, withdrew his Colt from the holster draped over the back of the chair, and tucked it snugly under his pillow.

Peeling off his britches and then his longjohns, he crawled in under the sheets. Once he was still, his weary eyes studying the ceiling, he became aware of the steady sound of activity in the street below. Snake Flat was obviously not a town that went to bed early. Occasionally a shot sounded somewhere, and every now and then there was an explosion of hoofbeats as a crowd of cowpunchers rode past.

Gradually the town quieted, and Longarm found himself going over in his mind once again that very interesting and informative proposal from Ogden Maxwell. The man had as good as given him a diagram of the forces loose in this town and the surrounding valley. He might have taken Maxwell's offer, of course, but if he had, he would have been allied so openly with those forces fighting Jake Telford, it would have been impossible for him to get any information from the man, certainly not the willing admission that he was, in truth, that famous train robber the federal government and the Pinkertons were after— Babe Warner.

In addition, there was much about Ogden Maxwell that Longarm did not especially like: an oiliness, an indefinable something that had put Longarm on guard from the moment Maxwell sat down at his table. If Ogden were selling horses, Longarm would look long and hard at any horseflesh he presented to him for sale. And even after he had satisfied himself that there was absolutely nothing wrong with the horse, he would still be unable to buy it. Ogden Maxwell was that kind of man.

But throwing in with Telford would not be easy. Not now. Not after Longarm's fatal rendezvous with one of his allies, Hank Dennim. Still, if the news of Longarm's refusal to join forces with Maxwell just now were to spread all the way to Telford, it might enable Longarm to approach Telford later, when the dust had settled.

For, as Longarm saw things now, he would have no choice but to seek out the Dennims and try to square himself one way or the other before they rode in and sought him out. The only problem was how Longarm could square himself with the Dennims without antagonizing Telford even further. Longarm sighed. He had ridden into a hornets' nest, as usual.

Footsteps approached his door, then paused.

Longarm reached under his pillow and closed his hand around his Colt's butt. There was a light rap on the door. He hauled out the .44, then flung back the covers and padded on bare feet over to the door.

"Who is it?"

"Rose," came the soft whisper.

"Rose, I ain't decent."

She laughed softly. "How long must I stand out here?"

Longarm considered, then shrugged. What the hell, he'd *told* her, hadn't he? He unlocked the door and pulled it open.

Rose slipped in and Longarm closed the door behind her.

"I am sorry to disturb your sleep," Rose told him, apparently not in the least upset by Longarm's naked figure standing palely before her in the darkened room.

"Hell, don't give it another thought," he told her, moving back to the bed and dropping his .44 into his holster. "I wasn't getting any shuteye. This town is a wild one."

"Yes," she said, walking closer to him. "It certainly is."

Rose was wearing fluffy bedroom slippers and a long pink cotton nightgown. She had combed out her auburn hair so that it spilled down past her shoulders.

"Is there . . . something you want, Rose?"

She sat down on the bed beside him. In the dimness, her eyes seemed to have grown to twice their size, and were as luminous as pools. "I want to apologize," she said.

"For what?"

"For judging you too harshly this afternoon."

"Why the sudden change in attitude?" Longarm asked, making no attempt to hide his skepticism.

"I don't blame you for being suspicious. May I explain?"

"I'm listening."

"At first I thought you acted too hastily, shooting that highwayman down like that. The awful, terrible suddenness of it left me confused and not a little dismayed. But this evening, as I dressed for my performance and peered at myself in the mirror, I leaned forward. There was a momentary ache in my stomach where that brute you shot down had punched me. And then I remembered the look in his eyes when he snatched that brooch from around my neck. He was an animal, and I see now that you killed him because you had no choice. He gave you no choice."

"That's about the way I see it, too," Longarm agreed.

"I was too quick to judge—too quick to accuse and turn away from the very man who had saved me. Now I am ashamed."

"No need for that. I can understand how you felt.

No one likes the hangman, but if it weren't for him, we'd all have to be carrying nooses around with us."

"Yes," she said. "Exactly." She leaned closer and took his hand in hers. "Then you do accept my apology?"

He leaned close enough for the scent she was wearing to fog his senses. Her arms moved up and closed about his shoulders. He leaned close and they kissed, her passionate mouth yielding deliciously to his probing lips. He pushed her gently down onto the bed. With a sigh, she embraced him, pulling him down upon her, her mouth working with a skill and deviltry that set Longarm afire.

They paused for a moment while he helped her slip out of the nightgown. For his own part, he had no such encumbrance. He closed his mouth over hers again, then eased her gently under him. When she felt his erection, she moaned softly, telling him how good it felt to feel a man this close and how long it had been for her. He moved his face down onto her lush, full breasts and closed his lips about her nipples, flagellating them gently with the tip of his tongue.

It drove her wild. She began thrusting herself up at him, moving in great sinuous waves as her entire body twisted and undulated beneath him like a giant snake. He let his lips pass lightly down over her belly, then further, down to the lips of her vagina. Crying out softly, she caught his head in both her hands and ground upward.

Laughing, he moved his lips back up her body, passing through her deep, sweaty cleft, then fastening his lips to the flesh under her ears, easing himself onto her as he did so. He felt her loins yawning hungrily open for him. Her fiery hands grabbed his erection and guided him. He felt himself slipping into her searing wetness, then plunged in deep and still deeper. She clung to him, pulling all of him into her, as deep as she could get him, moaning softly, her head moving to and fro.

"Yes . . . yes!" she told him. "Oh, yes! Oh, it feels so good inside me. So *good!*"

She was responding like a she-cougar in heat by now, digging her nails into his back and raising her knees until her ankles were crossed behind his neck. He was hitting bottom with every stroke until he eased off, afraid he might be hurting her.

But this only infuriated her. "All of it!" she muttered fiercely. "I want every inch of it inside me!"

That was all the encouragement he needed. Throwing caution to the winds, he began pounding into her with great, looping thrusts.

"Oh, my God!" she grunted a moment later. "I'm coming—coming again!"

He lost control then, and felt himself slipping over the edge. He pulled his head back and let loose, exploding deep within her, his erection pulsing repeatedly, coming fast and often.

Through it all, she clung to him fiercely, unwilling to let him withdraw. He did not argue as he stayed inside, impaling her on the bed as he grew large again. He heard her gasp with delight. Laughing softly himself, he pulled her over a bit on the bed for a more comfortable encounter, resting on his knees and taking his time as their heaving flesh got still better acquainted.

For a long, sweet time they clung to each other, rocking softly, letting it build slowly, deliciously. Then they were approaching the peak, climbing toward another climax. Their tempo increased. She began to moan and rake her nails down the length of his back. But he barely felt it as he increased the tempo. She started to cry out, then laugh. He was laughing himself now, and together they swept over the top, this time enjoying a long, shuddering mutual orgasm.

She went limp under him. He raised himself on his hands and grinned down at her. She smiled back up at him. Her face was gleaming with perspiration, and damp tendrils of hair were plastered to her forehead.

"Well, now, do you accept my apology?" she asked softly, a deep, throaty laugh breaking from her.

"Yes," he told her.

"Good. Now roll over. It's my turn."

Longarm rolled off her and lay back, spread-eagled, as she climbed atop him, resting a knee by each of Longarm's hip bones. She toyed with his moist erection with great patience until, to his surprise, he felt himself growing again. He laughed in amazement. Triumphant, her eyes glowing, she guided herself down onto him with both hands. As she leaned back suddenly and impaled herself on his erection, he sighed with pleasure. Laughing delightedly, she began rocking forward and back, gently, happily.

He just lay back and let her have her way with

him. It was pleasant, so pleasant. And then, surprisingly, he felt himself building to a climax once again. She, too, began to pant with mounting excitement. Abruptly, she leaned forward over him, swinging her nipples across his face.

"Suck it!" she cried. "Suck it!"

Reaching up for her breast, he guided it into his mouth.

Still riding him hard, she keened softly, happily as he sucked hard on her nipple. She gasped and cried out. Then he felt a shudder tremble through her. For a moment he was afraid she was going to come too soon and pull out. He reached down with both hands, grabbed her pelvis, and began slamming her down upon him with a sudden, wild ferocity.

An instant later, gasping, they both came in one long, exhausting, depleting orgasm. This time, her body covered with perspiration, she collapsed forward down onto his massive chest, clinging to him happily.

"Oh, my," she said softly, kissing the coiled hair on his chest. "I think that should do me for a good long time. But I am afraid I have made my hunger shamelessly apparent to you."

He laughed softly, pulled her over beside him, then kissed her. She returned his kiss. After a moment they parted, and she lay back on one of his pillows, sighing.

"I would like to stay here with you tonight," she told him.

"Then why don't you?"

She laughed. "It wouldn't be proper."

A footstep paused outside the door. Longarm came alert at once and started to turn. He was not fast enough. The door slammed open and Lucky Farrell burst into the room.

"I thought I heard that laugh of yours," he snarled.

Longarm could not be sure in the darkened room, but he thought he saw a gun in the man's hand. With a gasp, Rose sat up, pulling the sheets up over her bosom.

"Close the door if you're coming in," Longarm drawled.

Longarm knew where his Colt was—resting in his holster, which was looped over the chair at the foot of the bed. A helluva place for it to be at a time like this.

Farrell kicked the door shut.

"Lucky," Rose said, her voice trembling with barely controlled exasperation. "Get out of here. And if that's a gun in your hand put it down!"

"It's a gun," Farrell said.

"Look, Farrell," said Longarm, "this is a private party. And you weren't invited."

"That so?"

"Yes. And I think the lady is right. Put that gun down."

"I could put a bullet through your heart now. If I did, not a jury in the world would convict me."

"What the hell is that supposed to mean?"

"You have my wife in bed with you!"

"Oh, hell," Longarm muttered. He turned to Rose. "That true?"

"Yes."

"Why the hell didn't you tell me?"

"I didn't want to."

For most women, that was a good enough reason, Longarm realized. He looked back at Farrell. "So what now?"

Farrell's narrow shoulders appeared to slump. Longarm saw him thrust the gun he was carrying into his belt.

"Rose," he said, his voice ragged, "come out of here."

"Go ahead of me," she told him, her voice sharp with anger. "I'll see you back in the room."

"All right," Farrell said, his voice barely audible.

Farrell turned and left the room, closing the door softly behind him. Longarm flung himself from the bed, snatched up his Colt, and padded to the door. Turning the key in the lock, he looked back at Rose.

"I want an explanation," he said.

"Light the lamp," she told him, "and give me one of those cheroots you smoke."

He did as she suggested. A few moments later, both of them clothed somewhat, she sat wearily down beside him on the bed and told him that she had married Farrell because the two of them made such a fine team. Where she sang, he gambled, and both cleaned up handsomely.

She took a deep drag on the cheroot, expelling the smoke out through her nostrils, then went on.

Soon after their marriage, however, it became apparent they had a problem. Or rather, Farrell did. She was just too much of a woman for him, and he was not enough of a man for her. Though they tried mightily to solve the problem, they both realized eventually that there was no solution. Great partners though they

45

were in business, they made a very inept couple in bed.

Since that realization, they had both agreed that she was to be allowed to find what companionship she could, and he was to do the same—and neither one was to interfere with the other.

"It doesn't look to me as if he wants to keep the deal," Longarm observed.

"I know," she sighed. "It has not been an easy arrangement for him to keep. For that reason, I have remained more or less faithful to him for more than a year." She looked at Longarm and smiled sadly. "But I am afraid that when I saw you stride into the Bagdad this evening, I knew I was just not cut out to be a nun—and that I wasn't really angry with you after all."

Longarm shrugged and got up, went over to the door, and unlocked it. "Good night, Rose."

She got up from the bed and walked over to the door. Pausing beside him, she said, "Lucky usually spends the night gambling. I guess tonight he left his table early. I'm sorry, Custis."

"Don't be."

She started through the door. Suddenly he reached out and took her arm, restraining her. "Do you think you can trust him? He sounded pretty wild there for a moment. And he does have a gun, don't forget."

"Don't worry," she replied wearily. She kissed Longarm lightly on the lips. "This is not the first time. I can handle him." She slipped out the door.

Longarm closed it behind her and walked over to the dresser. He was cupping his hand about the chimney to blow out the lamp when he heard the shot. It came from one of the rear rooms—and the instant he heard it, he realized how wrong Rose Gantry had been.

She could not handle Lucky Farrell. Not this night.

Chapter 3

Frantically yanking on his Levi's, Longarm reached Rose's room just ahead of a small crowd of night-shirted guests. Rose was not dead. She was sitting up in an upholstered chair, her face as white as a pillow-case, one hand held up to her shoulder. Through her fingers trickled a steady stream of blood.

Longarm spun around and saw the desk clerk pushing his way into the room. "Get a doctor," Longarm told him. "Miss Gantry's been shot!"

The clerk spun about and vanished from the room. Longarm heard him running down the hall toward the stairs, then hurried over to Rose.

"Let me look at it," he said.

She pulled her hand away.

"What did he use?" he asked, as he leaned forward

to examine the ugly flesh wound. The bullet, apparently of a small calibre, had passed through the fleshy part of her shoulder.

"A pocket Smith and Wesson," she replied.

"What calibre?"

"Twenty-two, I think."

He felt a lot better. Straightening, he smiled encouragingly at Rose. "You're going to live."

"Custis, you must help me. What if Lucky tries again?"

"I won't let him, Rose."

Rose closed her eyes and appeared to relax. "That's good enough for me," she said.

Then she fainted.

As Longarm carried Rose over to her bed, the doctor pushed through the crowd outside the door and entered the room. With him came the town constable. Recalling Maxwell's dismissal of the man, Longarm could not help but agree. Lester Boggs was the kind of man who peered nervously at a doorframe whenever he passed through one. His chin was nonexistent and his blue eyes were watery.

"What happened?" the town constable asked.

Longarm walked over and closed the door. "Miss Gantry was shot by Lucky Farrell."

"Farrell?"

"Farrell's a gambler," Longarm explained. "He arrived today with Miss Gantry."

"Oh." Boggs looked unhappily past Longarm at the still unconscious Rose Gantry.

Longarm did, also. The doctor, a spare, gray-haired

man with a Vandyke beard, had rolled up his sleeves and was working quickly and deftly as he cut away Rose's nightdress.

Glancing at Boggs, Longarm said, "I think maybe you better stay outside Miss Gantry's door tonight, in case Farrell comes back."

Boggs swallowed nervously and began to sweat. "Sure," he said. "Good idea. You . . . think he'll come back?"

"I dont know. But I suggest you deputize someone to spell you."

The man brightened at once. "Sure. That's a good idea. No sense in me stayin' out in front of that door all night."

"Nope. Sure isn't. But I wouldn't leave Miss Gantry unguarded if I were you."

Longarm turned then and pulled open the door.

"Say," Boggs asked uncertainly, "where you goin', mister . . . ?"

"Name's Long. Custis Long. I'm going to look around outside. I know what this gambler looks like."

Pleased that it would be Longarm and not him going after the culprit, Boggs nodded so eagerly he looked like a spaniel who had just been given a pat on the head.

Longarm left the room, pushed through the patrons still remaining outside the door, and hurried back to his room to get dressed. It did not take him long to accomplish this, and in less than fifteen minutes, his saddle riding on his left shoulder and his rifle and the rest of his gear depending from his right hand, Longarm stepped out onto the hotel porch.

A large crowd on the porch was gathered about the desk clerk, who was giving the members of the crowd all the savory details. As the clerk spoke, there were outraged shouts and angry outbursts from several of the listeners, but no action as far as Longarm could discern.

He pushed his way through the crowd and started across the street toward the livery stable.

"Mr. Long!"

Longarm turned. A gray-haired man who had been approaching the hotel had turned and was hurrying toward him. Longarm waited for the man to catch up to him. His riding boots and attire marked him as a rancher rather than a townsman.

"What can you tell me about Miss Gantry?" the man asked. "Is she going to be all right?"

Longarm strode on across the street, the rancher keeping up with him. "The doc's with her now," he said. "It was only a flesh wound."

The man seemed mightily relieved. "Who did it?"

Longarm pulled up just outside the livery stable. "Lucky Farrell. He travels with Miss Gantry."

"That new gambler in town?"

"Yes."

"I lost a considerable sum to that man this evening," the man said.

"Sorry to hear that."

"It was my own fault, sir. I tried to stretch a full house a little too far for my own good." He smiled then. "Allow me to introduce myself. My name is Dan Saxon. I'm the owner of the Circle S."

Longarm took the man's offered hand. The grip was powerful. Despite the fact that he walked with a noticeable saddle-swagger, Saxon was tall and held himself erect, the stamp of many years peering into the wind and rain of the high country on his lean, aristocratic face. He was wearing a knee-length plantation-style coat and a string tie. His high-crowned Stetson he wore squarely, matching the level-headed directness of his gaze. Everything about him spoke of vast acres and a spawn of cattle to match.

"You own a spread here in this valley?" Longarm asked.

"Yes, I do," Saxon replied proudly. "My daughter Rita and I run it."

"From what I hear, there aren't many independent ranch holdings left in the valley."

Saxon nodded grimly. "I saw you talking to Ogden in the Bagdad. I suppose he's already explained to you what we're up against. Ogden's as concerned as I am." He looked closely at Longarm. "I don't mind telling you, I'm disappointed he was not able to convince you to throw in with us."

"If it had been you and not Ogden doing the talking, I might have considered the offer more seriously."

"Ogden sometimes comes on too strongly, I must admit."

Longarm smiled coldly. "Yes, he does. And I didn't trust him. Still, that don't matter none, Saxon. The angel Gabriel couldn't have convinced me to get involved in a range war. Now, if you'll excuse me."

"Just a moment, Long. About Miss Gantry."

"Yes?"

"This gambler Farrell shot her, you say?" Saxon asked.

"He did."

"Is the man still running loose?"

"He is."

"Do you think he might try to harm Rose again?"

"There's a good chance he might," Longarm said.

"Well, shouldn't there be someone to guard her?"

"The town constable's up there now."

"Lester Boggs?" Saxon's voice betrayed his dismay.

"That's the man. I told him he might want someone to spell him later. Maybe you could handle that little chore."

Saxon brightened instantly. "Why, of course, Mr. Long. I'd be delighted to assist Miss Gantry." Saxon started across the street. "Much obliged, Mr. Long. I hope we meet again."

Watching him go, Longarm hoped he would. He liked Saxon. There was an honesty and a directness about his manner that impressed him—in stark contrast to Ogden Maxwell, the corpulent townsman Saxon had let speak for him.

Longarm turned and, still hefting his saddle and gear, walked through the wide-open stable door. The hostler was a stove-up cowboy with a face cured almost black by wind and sun. At the moment he was currying a large, deep-chested black near the stable door, obviously in order that he might be able to keep an eye on the crowd stomping up onto the hotel porch.

As Longarm entered the stable, he put down the

brush and straightened up. "You lookin' to rent a horse, mister?"

Longarm dumped his saddle on the floor and leaned his rifle against the side of a horse stall. "First, some questions. Did anyone come in here not long ago and rent a horse?"

"Nope." The hostler sent a black spear of tobacco juice into a pile of horse manure. "He didn't *rent* a horse. He slugged me over the head and stole one. He also took my rifle, an old Henry. Is he the one you're lookin' for?"

"A thin feller dressed in black?"

The hostler sent another thick gob of tobacco after the first. "That's the son of a bitch, all right. I been waiting for the town constable or someone to come askin' about him. You're the first one to do so."

"What's he riding?"

"A bay. He took one of my saddles, too."

"Which way did he go?"

"He tore off down the street, heading for the flats north of town. He was roweling that bay somethin' fierce."

"Then I'll be wanting a horse," Longarm said. "What about that black you were currying just now?"

"Sure. He's a fine animal. But ain't you goin' to wait for the posse?"

"What posse?"

"Ain't there one forming up? He shot that new singer in town, didn't he?" the hostler asked.

"Yes, he did."

"So I figured there'd be a posse formin' up."

"Where is it?"

The hostler poked his head out through the stable door and looked across the street at the crowd still milling excitedly about in front of the hotel. Occasionally, sharp barks of laughter broke from its midst. The shooting of a dance-hall singer was, after all, not all that heinous an offense.

The hostler ducked back into the stable and nodded somewhat sheepishly at Longarm. "You're right, mister. It'll be a cold day in hell before them damn fools get around to forming a posse."

"So let's saddle up that black," Longarm said.

Longarm lugged his saddle over to the black as the hostler went for reins and a bridle. As soon as the black was saddled, Longarm mounted up. But before he rode out of the stable, he glanced down at the hostler.

"What can you tell me about that horse Farrell took?"

The hostler smiled, revealing several black gaps in his yellow teeth. "You'll be lookin' fer sign—is that it?"

Longarm nodded.

The hostler moved closer and squinted up at Longarm through his white, bushy eyebrows. "That bay ain't lame, mind you. But he's got a corn on his right front hoof. Runs right across the hoof, it does. If you're trackin', you'll notice it as a bar across the hoofprint." The hostler spat out a huge gob of tobacco juice. "You can't miss it."

Longarm thanked the hostler, ducked his head, and clattered out of the stable.

Without a single glance back at the crowd still

milling in front of the hotel, he rode off down the street, heading north. He kept on through the night down the center of the valley, following a wide trail pounded down by many hoofs and wagon wheels. In the moonlight he occasionally caught the fresh print of new tracks.

Not long after daybreak, Longarm found himself riding parallel to a stream. In the soft mud beside the stream, he caught sight of a horse's hoofprints where Farrell had cut closer to it. Dismounting, Longarm studied the hoofprints and found what he was looking for: a right forefoot that left an imprint resembling a flattened A, the crossbar in the A formed by the ridge of the horse's corn.

Straightening up, Longarm looked around. Farrell had paused here to let his horse drink his fill, and since there were no more tracks on this side of the stream, that was a sure indication the gambler had decided to leave the trace and make for high country. Longarm studied the dim mountains to the west of him. Once in those foothills, Longarm realized, Farrell would have a better than even chance of getting away entirely.

Longarm let his horse drink, then mounted up and splashed across the stream. Like a finger pointing, the hoofprints of Farrell's horse headed straight for the foothills.

Before long, Longarm had lifted the black to a lope.

With only two hours of sunlight left, Longarm felt the country beginning to lift under him. Soon the monotonously level terrain of the valley floor began to give way to rolling dunes and sand and clay gulches. Here and there a pine tree stood as advance sentinel to the hills looming before him.

Still following Farrell's tracks, Longarm came to a shallow creek and dismounted. Again he found the hoofprint of the bay Farrell was riding. The print was close to the water's edge, and was quite clearly a recent one. No moisture had yet drained into it. Longarm swung back aboard his black, let the horse have a short drink, then pushed on into the benchlands.

Soon he was following a game trail that cut through a wilderness of massive boulders. Beyond the broken world in front of him, the dark bulk of the mountains thrust into the sky, closer now, formidable, great ramparts that seemed flung up before him as a warning.

An hour or so later, as he was riding at a steady trot through a steep-sided gorge, he caught the glint of a rifle barrel high in the rocks ahead of him. It was too late to turn back now. Clapping spurs to the black's flank, he lifted his horse to a hard gallop, waiting for the shot, gambling that when it came it would prove Farrell to be as bad a marksman as he was a murderer. When the shot came, the bullet ricocheted harmlessly off a boulder well behind him on the trail.

Encouraged, Longarm snatched the Winchester out of its boot, flung himself from the saddle, and slapped the black's rump. As the horse galloped into a pile of rocks off the trail, Longarm ducked behind a boulder and levered a cartridge into firing position. Another shot from above sent sharp echoes rebounding through the rocky gorge. This time, the ricochet came uncomfortably close. Longarm realized that Farrell had him pretty well bracketed.

Keeping down, he ducked out from behind the boulder and raced across the trail, holding in his mind a clear vision of the spot high in the rocks where he had caught the glint of Farrell's gun barrel. Zigzagging through a wilderness of scrub and huge, broken shards of rock, he reached a light stand of pine. Plunging into the timber, he kept going, and soon found himself angling up a steep slope. A hopeless, prayerful shot came from somewhere above him. The round whined futilely off the rocks below him.

Farrell had lost Longarm completely, and was shooting now simply to keep up his courage.

Longarm reached a ridge and raced along its crest. When he came to the end of it, he leaped down to a narrow game trail and followed it up the slope for about fifty more yards. Then he left it to race up a steep slope toward the narrow ledge where Farrell was perched. Longarm came to a cleft in the rockface that looked as if it would lead around behind the ledge. He ducked into it. As he did so, from the ledge above came another shot as Farrell continued to shoot at shadows on the trail below. Longarm removed his spurs and continued on through the cleft.

Once through it, he began to scale a series of giant granite slabs. Coming at last to one massive upthrust of rock, Longarm clambered up onto it, then raced swiftly up its steep back until he judged himself to be well above the ledge from which Farrell was still firing. Dropping to his belly, he inched his way across the surface of the rock slab until his head was barely peering over its edge.

Directly below him, at a distance of perhaps a hundred feet, Farrell was crouched, his rifle resting on a rock in front of him. The gambler had an unobstructed view of the trail as it sliced through the gorge. If he had been a better shot and had fired sooner, he could have picked off Longarm easily. Looking beyond Farrell at the trail below, Longarm could see his black cropping grass in among a tangle of boulders. Farrell's own bay was tied to a sapling in the rocks behind the gambler.

As Longarm eased his rifle into position, Farrell reached into his rear pocket and pulled out a whiskey bottle. Tipping it up, the gambler swallowed greedily, then stuck the bottle back into his pocket. Longarm saw now why the gambler's attempt at bushwhacking him had fared so poorly. Farrell was drunk.

"Farrell!" Longarm called down to him. "Drop your rifle!"

The man whirled, caught sight of Longarm, and flung up his rifle. Working his lever frantically, he fired up at Longarm. The slugs whined off the rockface beneath him as Longarm ducked back. When he looked over again, Farrell was scrambling back from the ledge, reaching for his horse's reins.

Longarm sighted quickly and fired. The shot missed Farrell and creased the bay's flank. The startled animal reared wildly and pulled the reins out of Farrell's grasp. Whinnying shrilly, the horse bolted. Racing after his horse, Farrell vanished underneath Longarm.

Pushing himself back from the edge of the rock, Longarm got to his feet and raced back down the boulder, then dropped to a narrow ledge and plunged swiftly down the slope. As soon as he reckoned himself below Farrell, he followed a narrow game trail that led back up the slope, coming at Farrell now from the direction his horse had taken.

The rapid clink of iron on stone caused Longarm to pull up and flatten himself against a rock. He was just in time as Farrell's horse bolted by him, nostrils flared, eyes wild. As soon as the horse was gone, Longarm continued up the narrow trail, his rifle ready.

A moment later, the chink of Farrell's spurs alerted him. Crouching low, Longarm moved to the side of the trail. Less than ten yards above him, Farrell broke into the clear, his eyes on the rocky trail in front of him as he scrambled after the bay's hoofprints.

"Drop the rifle, Farrell!"

The gambler did not have that much sense. He swung up the rifle, his eyes wild and desperate. Longarm fired up at him twice, pumping carefully each time. Dust puffed off Farrell's vest as two neat holes appeared in it. Farrell was hurled violently backward onto the game trail.

He did not move after he hit the ground.

Longarm climbed up the trail to him. The stench of cheap whiskey assailed Longarm's nostrils. Longarm realized the bottle in the gambler's back pocket must have shattered when he landed. Shaking his head, he looked down into the dead gambler's face, won-

61

Chapter 4

Three days later, Longarm was on hand to witness Rose Gantry's return to the Bagdad's small stage. When she stepped into view wearing a bright red dress, her left arm resting in a black silk sling, she received a thunderous welcome from the packed saloon.

Once again she sang of lonely cowboys mourning the girls they left behind. Though it was obvious to everyone in Snake Flat by this time that Rose Gantry did not resemble in the least any of those patient gals or lovesick cowpokes she sang about, it mattered little to her hushed, solemn audience. At the conclusion of her performance, their cheers kept Rose longer than she had intended, and for an encore she rendered a melting "Red River Valley" and followed that up with a spirited rendition of the "Zebra Dun." It brought the house down.

As the howling patrons kept cheering and stomping in an effort to bring Rose back on the stage for just one more song, a tall, rawboned cattleman pushed through the crowd and came to a halt beside Longarm's table.

"Howdy," the cattleman said, his sky-blue eyes squinting coolly down through the smoke at Longarm. "Mind if I join you?"

"It's a free country," Longarm replied.

"It is that," the cattleman responded, pulling a chair over and slumping into it.

An anxious bar girl had followed after him through the stomping crowd. She pulled up now beside their table and waited for the cattleman's order.

"What're you drinkin'?" he asked Longarm.

"Maryland rye."

The cattleman glanced up at the bar girl. "Maryland rye. Bring the bottle and a glass."

She turned and vanished into the crush.

"My name's Jake Telford," the cattleman said, holding out his hand.

Longarm took his hand and shook it. The clasp was strong, the hands callused from years of handling a rope. "Long," Longarm said. "Custis Long."

"Pleased to meet you, Long. Been hearin' things."

"All good, I hope."

The girl brought the Maryland rye and set the bottle and glass down on the table before Telford. He paid her handsomely. Her eyes lit up and she darted back

64

the way she had come. Telford poured the rye into his glass.

"Cheers," he said, lifting the glass.

Longarm lifted his own and the two drank.

"You throw a wide loop," Telford commented amiably. "A one-man vigilante group."

Longarm shrugged.

"I like a man knows how to take care of himself. Trouble is, I got friends who had to go searching for one of their kin you dumped by a roadside."

Longarm smiled. "That means you got friends who earn their keep robbing stages."

"They didn't earn much this time," Telford admitted ruefully, smiling back at Longarm.

"I gather I was supposed to stand still for that raise?"

"Hell, no. But you could've brought the body in. Dumped him in the stage boot, maybe."

"Hank would've been just as dead. Besides, I suggested to the jehu he should send someone back for the body."

"That was right thoughtful of you."

In Ned Buntline's *Wild West* magazine, road agents and train robbers were portrayed as pretty fine fellows, a cheerful, adventurous lot, any one of whom a man would be proud to claim as a friend. But Longarm had never met one who impressed him all that much. For the most part they were a mean-looking, shifty-eyed bunch who drank their food and seldom shaved or cut their hair—a filthy lot who counted on a summer cloudburst for their annual bath. Most of them had difficulty making their mark, and only a few could read without moving their lips. Though they were sometimes bright enough to come in out of the rain, they often had to give the matter considerable thought.

But, as Longarm studied Telford, he was considerably impressed by the man's bearing—the easy, soft-spoken power that emanated from him. If this was the famous Babe Warner, who had made his fortune robbing trains and stagecoaches, he simply did not look the type. He was as lean and rangy as a Texas steer. His eyes were alert, his long, angular face clean-shaven, his thick white hair combed neatly and trimmed to the collar. His range clothes were expensive but not flashy. And, rough though his hands were, his nails were immaculate. Indeed, everything about the man was clean and sharply cut. There were no ragged edges.

"It appears to me," Longarm said carefully, "that those three friends of yours should've gone to school on how to rob a stage. For one thing, they didn't seem to know the stagecoach wasn't carrying a strongbox, only passengers. And they let me take them completely by surprise."

"They weren't thinking too clearly, I admit. It was a fool operation from the start. I guess maybe the Dennims have had their way too much around here. They were careless."

"Carelessness can be a fatal disease."

"Indeed it can, Long." He smiled. "That's why I stopped over here for this little chat. I think it would be careless of you to remain any longer in this valley."

"That's one way of putting it."

"You can do what you want, of course. I just thought I'd let you know. Pa Dennim and his boys only just buried Hank yesterday. Soon's they gather themselves back together, I figure one or the other of them'll ride in here to square things."

"Let 'em ride in. It's a free country."

"So it is, Long. So it is. But Pa and me go back a ways. I wouldn't want to see anything bad happen to him."

Longarm shrugged. "Something bad already has. I suggest you might do better convincing Pa Dennim to keep his boys at home."

"Afraid they wouldn't listen—to Pa or me."

Longarm leaned back in his chair and regarded Telford coolly. "And what makes you think I'd listen, Telford?"

"You seem like a reasonable man."

"How so?"

"You've already shown good sense. I happen to know you refused to throw in with Ogden Maxwell. He offered you the town marshal job. As the town marshal—and later the sheriff—you could have made things hot around here. But you had the good sense to turn down Ogden's offer. You refused Dan Saxon, too, I understand."

"That I did."

"So why not ride out?"

"I like the valley," Longarm drawled. He smiled. "The air is clean. There ain't any cities nearby to fog the senses. And maybe I'd like to buy me a small ranch here and settle down. Like you did."

Telford looked at Longarm sharply for a moment.

Then he shrugged and got to his feet. "I just thought you deserved a warning, Long."

"And I appreciate it, Telford."

He nodded brusquely and left, striding through the crowd, which opened before him like the Red Sea before Moses. Jake Telford was a big man in these parts. And, despite himself, Longarm liked the man.

Backstage, Longarm greeted Rose Gantry and Dan Saxon. Since the night Dan had taken it upon himself to station himself as a personal guard outside Rose Gantry's room, he had been riding in from his ranch each evening to see to her needs. Now Saxon was helping Rose push her way through a crowd of well-wishers which had congregated outside her tiny dressing room. Rose, all smiles, appeared to be hanging on to Saxon's arm for dear life. Accompanying her father this night was Rita Saxon. She had met Longarm only briefly earlier that evening. She greeted him now with a smile that seemed unusually warm.

"Long," Saxon said, as they were descending the saloon's rear porch, "Rita here thinks you ought to take my offer and become the town marshal."

"Yes, I do," said Rita, taking Longarm's arm and gazing up at him with eyes that fairly sparkled. "I think you would do nicely."

"You want me to get my head shot off? Is that it, Miss Rita?"

"No one would dare!"

Rose and Saxon laughed. By this time they were heading toward the hotel, keeping to the back alley. It was the only way Rose could return to her room without having to plow her way through a crowd of cheering railroad men or cowpokes.

When they reached the hotel, Dan Saxon suggested to Rose that she might like to relax on the porch with him and his daughter for a while before going up to her room. Rose agreed with a smile. Longarm tipped his hat to Rose, bid good night to Rita, and went on into the hotel and up to his room.

He had just finished lighting the lamp on his dresser when there came a light rap on his door. He withdrew his Colt and moved back to the door. Standing to one side of it, he asked, "Yes? Who's there?"

"It's me. Rita."

Longarm lowered his gun and opened the door.

"My, you *are* careful, aren't you?" she said as she stepped into his room.

He holstered the Colt and closed the door behind her. She walked into the room as far as the foot of his bed, then turned to face him, an uncertain smile on her face.

"Yes," he said, "I am careful. It's the careful ones who get to go to other men's funerals."

She shuddered. "What a grim way of putting it."

Longarm shrugged and walked toward her, frowning. "I am sorry. I don't have the tongue of a poet, it seems. What can I do for you, Miss Rita?"

"First of all, you can stop that 'Miss' business, and just call me by my first name."

He smiled. "As you wish."

In the lamplight, she looked mighty pretty. Her soft olive skin and eyes reminded Longarm of lazy Texas towns and sultry, starlit nights along the Rio

Grande. She moved gracefully, and her smile was warm and inviting.

"Did your father come from Texas?" Longarm asked.

Her smile was dazzling. "Yes. And my mother was Spanish. I am pleased that you noticed."

"It would be hard not to."

"My father came a long way to find a home in this valley, Mr. Long. My mother died giving birth to me in this high, lonely country. And now I am standing here before you to do what my father failed to do— to convince you to side with him and those of us in the valley who still have enough backbone left to stand up to Jake Telford."

"And just how do you propose I do that? Become the town marshal and then go after Telford at the head of a posse?"

"No. When Dad told me what Maxwell proposed, I disagreed. We shouldn't try to buy our own law. But the Circle S needs a good hand, Mr. Long."

"And you're making me an offer?"

"Forty a month and found," she said. "Moving a bunch of cattle up into the hills, then down again in the spring. Long hours and hard ones." She walked to the window and looked out over the dark huddle of the town at two twin peaks due west looming into the bright, moonlit sky. "Our ranch is in the lap of those two peaks, Mr. Long. It's high country, but beautiful country. And that means cold camps and early risings and no pay till the job is done. And I am afraid that won't be until we've managed somehow to outlast Telford's gang of cutthroats."

"Is that your offer?"

"There's more," she said, turning to face him, her eyes glinting suddenly. "I will do all in my power to make your employment at the Circle S . . . pleasant."

He laughed teasingly. "When I'm not up in the hills, that is, tryin' to get warm in them cold camps you mentioned."

He was treating her lightly, too lightly, and he could see the angry light that leapt into her eyes. She pulled up short and tipped her head. "Whatever is amusing is only amusing to you, I am afraid."

He sobered. "Sorry I laughed, Rita. That wasn't kind of me, I admit."

"Nevertheless, you are . . . refusing my offer."

"As I told your father, I am not interested in getting caught up in this undeclared war between Maxwell and Telford."

"Telford spoke to you in the saloon tonight. I saw him."

"It's a free country."

"You mean you did not agree to throw in with him?"

"No, I did not."

She looked at him for a long moment, as if she were trying to decide whether or not to believe him.

"Rita," he told her, "he joined me at my table to warn me. He told me to get out of Snake Flat and the valley. He as much as implied my life wasn't worth a plugged nickel with the Dennims gunning for me."

She frowned. "And are you going to leave the valley?"

"No."

"Then what *are* you going to do?"

"This."

He closed the distance between them, lifted her off her feet, and swung her into his arms. Then he turned and crossed to the bed and dropped her lightly down onto the coverlet. Smiling, he leaned over, his hands braced on either side of her, and kissed her on the lips. She fought the kiss for only an instant; then her mouth softened, opened, and she flung her arms around his neck and pulled him down onto her.

There was a freshness about her lips, an innocent eagerness in her passion that startled him. He pulled back quickly and looked down at her flushed face. "Rita, are you a virgin?"

"Why should that matter?"

He sat back and gently unwound her arms from around his neck.

"I think I'd better go downstairs to cool off," he told her, standing up.

He walked to the door, opened it, and went out into the hall. He was still shaking his head when he stepped out onto the cool veranda a moment later and found himself a wicker chair against the wall.

When Rita hurried from the hotel a few minutes later, he was puffing contentedly on a cheroot. Looking neither to the right nor the left, she descended the porch steps and started across the street to the livery stable where her father had left their buggy.

Longarm had no doubt Rita was aware of him sitting in the shadows on the veranda, smoking his cheroot. But she was too upset and embarrassed to look his way. As he watched her go, her back ramrod-straight, her chin lifted defiantly, Longarm wondered for a moment if he had done the right thing. Rita's pride had certainly taken a beating. Undoubtedly she had imagined herself a most delectable prize. Still, Longarm would rather injure her pride than take advantage of her desperate need to help her father.

Even as he was thinking this, Dan Saxon left the hotel and hurried across to the livery after his daughter. Glancing toward the door, Longarm saw Rose Gantry standing on the veranda, well back in the shadows, watching the cattleman go into the livery.

A moment later, as the buggy left town with Dan Saxon driving, Rose left the shadows and walked over to Longarm. Sitting down in a wicker chair next to him, she smiled. In the darkness, her teeth gleamed like pearls.

"Dan's very nice," she said.

"A decent man," Longarm agreed.

She was silent for a while, then she spoke up. "Is there any reason why you won't help Dan?"

"So far, I don't see he needs it," Longarm drawled. "He's doin' just fine all by himself."

She laughed softly, her voice deep and musical. "That's not what I meant, Custis, and you know it."

Longarm lit up another cheroot. "Give me time to look over the ground before I stake a claim," he said. "This feller Telford doesn't seem like such a bad one. And I sure as hell was not impressed by Ogden Maxwell."

"Dan has notes outstanding in Telford's bank. Telford has made no secret he wants Dan's spread. He needs the water rights for his herds."

"And he's threatening to call in Dan's notes?"

"Yes."

"That's his right, isn't it?"

"You think Dan should sell to Telford? Give Telford the entire valley?"

"Hell, Rose, I didn't tell Dan to go into debt. He signed them notes all by his lonesome."

"Yes, I suppose you're right."

"Is Telford offering Dan a fair price for his spread?" Longarm asked.

"I am sure he thinks he is."

"But Dan doesn't."

"The ranch is his life."

"I am not my brother's keeper, Rose."

"I don't think the man who tracked down Lucky Farrell believes that," she said.

"I did not intend to kill him, Rose. But when I told him to drop his weapon, he opened up on me. He seemed determined to have me kill him."

"He was a fool. I never loved him and he never loved me. But he had come to believe I was his property."

Longarm did not bother to respond as he leaned back in the chair and puffed on his cheroot. He would never get used to the cold ruthlessness a woman could exhibit when it came to the disposal of a lover.

After a moment, Rose got to her feet.

"Good night, Custis."

"Good night, Rose."

She vanished into the hotel while he remained in his chair and finished smoking his cheroot. As he did so, he went over in his mind once again the difficulty of his present assignment. He had to find out for sure if this man Jake Telford was in truth Babe Warner—and in such a way that his evidence would stand up in court. Short of walking up to Telford and asking him point-blank where he got all the money he used to buy up most of the valley, Longarm had not the foggiest notion of how he was going to get that evidence.

His best bet was still for him somehow to become the man's confidant. Yet everything that had been happening to him since he arrived made such an alliance virtually impossible.

He flung his cheroot into the darkness and got to his feet. He felt too restless to retire for the night. Descending the porch steps, he started down the street on his way to the saloon for a nightcap. He was moving across the mouth of an alley when he caught a sound behind him. Swinging about, he caught a furtive movement in the alley's yawning blackness.

At once he recalled Telford's warning and ducked low.

From the alley's mouth came the flat crash of a Colt .45. Longarm felt the air-lash of the bullet, and a second later a window across the street disintegrated. Drawing his own Colt, he kept low and crabbed swiftly behind the corner of the blacksmith shop. A couple of blocks down, a crowd broke from the saloon, shouting excitedly. Longarm paid no heed.

From deeper within the alley, the gun fired again. This second bullet slammed into the shingles just above

Longarm's head. His eyes riveted to a spot just above the gunflash, Longarm aimed quickly and fired. There was no return fire.

Abruptly, Longarm heard the sudden pounding of retreating feet as the bushwhacker made a break for it.

Jumping up, Longarm plunged into the alley, leaping to one side as he did so. He was just in time. A sixgun thundered from the rear of the alley, the gunman firing at the spot where Longarm had been an instant before. The lancing flash of gunpowder momentarily turned the alley bright as day. Longarm fired twice in rapid succession at the gunflash.

This time a gasp of pain cut through the reverberating silence, and a shadowy figure bolted around the corner and disappeared into the back alley. Longarm darted after him. The back alley was as black as a whore's heart. After a few minutes, wary of trash barrels and heaped debris, he slowed down and drifted over to the shadows cast by the buildings. Crouching low, he kept going. A privy loomed out of the night to his right. He heard a hinge creak and flung up his gun. A pale figure materialized in the privy doorway. A gun barrel gleamed.

Longarm fired twice, slamming the pale figure back into the outhouse. Something heavy and metallic struck the floor of the privy. Cautiously, his Colt held out warily in front of him, Longarm moved into the outhouse.

The man he assumed was one of the Dennim brothers had fallen back and was lying face up across the two privy holes. Peering close, Longarm was able to make out the wide, staring whites of the man's eyes. He looked—and smelled—very dead. Longarm's foot struck the dead man's dropped sixgun. Longarm picked it up and stuck it into his belt.

Then he turned and left the dead bushwhacker in the outhouse, where he belonged.

Longarm was sitting at a small table in the saloon, his back to the wall. The doctor had just been in to tell him it was Will Dennim he had killed. Will had suffered a flesh wound in the thigh, but the two bullets that finished him had crashed into his chest. One ranged up into his lungs, the other into his heart, where they had lodged. Will had died almost instantly, the doctor told Longarm.

The patrons began drifting back into the saloon. Longarm watched them morosely. He noticed how, as the men eased their bellies up against the bar, each one managed to cast a curious, even furtive glance at Longarm's solitary figure.

Longarm poured himself another drink. He was not drunk, and he was determined he would not get soused. It was a luxury he could no longer afford. He was just using the tonsil varnish to gentle himself down.

He looked up to see Jake Telford, a fresh bottle and a glass in his hand, approaching his table.

Telford pulled up. "Mind if I join you?"

"Sit down. And welcome."

Telford slacked his long figure into the chair across the table from Longarm and filled his glass. "You got a wildcat by the tail," he observed.

Longarm nodded.

77

"What do you propose to do now?"

"Keep on swinging the wildcat. I can't let the son of a bitch down now, can I?"

"You could ride out of here."

"Sure. With my tail between my legs. I'm not running, Telford."

Telford leaned back in his chair and regarded Longarm shrewdly. "No," he said, "I didn't think you would."

"I can be grateful for one thing," Longarm said.

"What's that?"

"All them Dennims didn't come after me at the same time."

"The Dennims have a crude sense of honor."

Longarm grinned. "Some honor. They wouldn't come at me together, but nothing stopped Will from trying to bushwhack me from a dark alley."

Telford smiled thinly. "I said it was crude."

"Yes. So you did."

Telford looked at Longarm for a long moment, then appeared to come to a decision. "Long, I have a suggestion. And I wish you would give it serious consideration."

"I'm listening."

"You told me you liked this valley. That you wanted to buy a place here. Settle down, maybe, like I did. That right?"

"That's what I said."

"All right, then. Join me. If you do, I'll let you run the Saxon ranch for me. It's the prettiest spread in the valley."

"The Circle S?"

"That's right. I'm foreclosing on it next week."

"Saxon know this?"

"He knows."

"You think he'll let you take his land?"

"Of course he won't let me. That's why I'd like your gun on our side. We'll need all the help we can get. From what I hear, Saxon's organizing the rest of the ranchers in the valley."

"And you want me to throw in with you against them?"

"That's what I said."

"What makes you think I'd do that?"

"Because I figure you're ridin' the owlhoot trail right now yourself." He leaned back and waited for Longarm's denial. When it didn't come, he smiled and went on. "And so maybe you could use a place to hole up."

"Now what would give you the idea I was on the run?"

"I ain't heard of you before this, Long. But you ain't foolin' me none. I know why you turned up in Snake Flat. It ain't just the climate. Word gets around about a place like this. You're on the dodge—and Snake Flat's a place where you heard you could lay low for a while. Ain't that right?"

Longarm shrugged and continued to sip his whiskey.

Telford chuckled. "I like a man who can keep his mouth shut, Long. You don't have to tell me nothing. I understand. But the thing is, once we get this valley, you can all start over. No more dry camps. No more lookin' over your shoulder. Hell, I'll let you run the

Circle S. You can run my brand on it, and maybe a few of your own."

"Your brand?"

"The T Bar," Telford replied, not without considerable pride. "Just ride out of town a ways. You'll see that brand most everywhere."

"What about the Dennims?"

"Stay clear of them. Let me see what I can do to calm things down."

"That's a tall order."

"Pa'll see things my way when I explain it to him."

"Sure he will. For a while. But I would never be able to turn my back on Bo or the old man. And there'd come a time when one of them would try to even the score."

"I told you. Just leave them to me."

"No. I'd join you, Telford, if I could trust the Dennims. But I can't."

Telford leaned heavily back in his chair, his eyes going suddenly bleak. "And that's your final word."

"Yes."

"You're going after Pa and Bo?"

Longarm shrugged. "I'm going to ride out and talk to them. See if I can explain things. If not, I'll have to deal with them. I don't see any other way."

"There is. Let me handle it."

"No. This is my show, Telford. I don't send anyone on my errands."

Telford got to his feet and looked down at Longarm. "I'm sorry, Long," the man said. "I sure am. Go out and talk to Pa if you want. Just don't hurt the old son of a bitch or I'll come lookin' for you myself. That's a promise."

"I told you. I'm just going out there to talk sense to the man. He's got one son left. He might like to settle for that."

"You'll find it a hell of a lot easier to ride into Pa's spread than to ride out once he learns who you are."

"Then I'll just have to cross that bridge when I come to it, won't I?"

"Yes, you will."

Telford turned on his heel and left the saloon. Longarm poured himself a glass of whiskey and downed it quickly. It should have made him feel better, but it didn't.

He had come here to join Telford and his gang. A moment before, Telford had given him a chance to throw in with him, and he had refused. How in hell could he ride into the Circle S alongside Telford, throwing lead and grinning like a possum chewing yellowjackets, while Telford's men dragged Rita and her father from the cabin.

For that was what it would come to, finally: a range war, with no holds barred. And Longarm could not see how Saxon and the rest of the ranchers would be any match at all for Jake Telford and his gang of outcasts.

Chapter 5

Longarm did not sleep in his hotel room that night. And the first light of dawn found him aboard the black, heading northeast. He was following the hostler's directions to the Dennim's spread, the Lazy D. The hostler had described it as a scattering of buildings in the lee of a bluff a full day's ride from Snake Flat.

Longarm's purpose was to do what he had told Telford he must do: inform Pa Dennim and Will's brother Bo that he wanted to end this fool gunplay. He saw no sense in letting this thing hang fire until Bo and his old man were ready to come after him some night from the mouth of another dark alley. Longarm's plan was simple and direct. He would explain matters to Pa Dennim and ask the man to bury the hatchet. If he refused, the fat would be in the fire—and Longarm would proceed to cross that bridge he had mentioned to Telford.

It was a gamble, of course. There was always the chance Longarm would not leave the Dennim spread alive. But he did not see any alternative—not if he were to be left alive long enough to collar Jake Telford, that is.

Soon he found himself riding over a fair, sun-drenched land that undulated gently all the way to the distant hills. The grass was lush, lusher than he had seen it in Colorado or Wyoming, good range with cattle already heavy with tallow feeding on it, all of them carrying T Bar brands, just as Telford had boasted to Longarm the night before. There were few fences and Longarm rode easily, unhurriedly. He was in no hurry to reach the Dennims and he liked riding across this bright land with the nearly cloudless sky arching over his head, the pine-stippled hills drawing ever nearer. Meadowlarks called and wild roses danced elegantly in the light, fragrant wind. It was a relief to be done, for a while at least, with the cramped ugliness of Snake Flat.

Late that afternoon, the dim trace Longarm had been following passed through the Lazy D's gate. It was in need of repair, he noted. The bleached long-horn skull nailed to the crossboard had had both its eye sockets blasted out by the guns of playful cow-pokes, and the gate itself sagged so crookedly on its hinges that it hung permanently open, weeds anchoring it to the valley floor. A half-hour later he was riding through scrub-covered hills and, not long after, the Lazy D's ranch buildings came in sight. They were log and frame structures, their backsides hiked up against the raw, weathered face of a low bluff.

Longarm pulled up for a moment on the crest of a low hill to gaze at the gaunt, oversized ranch house with its long, unpainted veranda and the low, sod-roofed bunkhouse, the barns and corrals and blacksmith shop. A few saddle horses stomped in the corrals, their tails switching idly at flies. No woodsmoke lifted from the cookshack chimney. The place appeared to be deserted.

Longarm nudged the black on down the hill and rode into the front yard, dismounted, and led his horse to the watering trough, careful to let it drink only a little at a time. He knew for sure the ranch was not deserted—that the Dennims would make their presence known when it suited them.

He was reaching for the pump handle when he caught a sudden movement out of the corner of one eye. Glancing over, he saw a tall, lanky fellow step into view in the barn doorway, a rifle in his hand. A second later, a footfall from behind alerted him. He turned carefully around. A girl was stepping out from behind the blacksmith shop, a double-barrelled Greener in her hands.

"Hold it right there, mister," the girl told him, her voice sharp and uncompromising.

"That's the one, Terry!" cried the fellow standing in the barn doorway. "I swear to God that's the bastard. He's the one shot down Hank!"

Longarm glanced quickly back at him. This had to be the surviving brother, Bo Dennim. He was as lanky as the girl, and his face had the same wolflike leanness

85

as his two brothers. He needed a haircut and a shave. His Levi's were spattered with patches of dry horse manure, and the white undershirt he wore under his yellow braces was stained and torn.

"That true, mister?" the girl wanted to know. "You the one killed Hank?"

Longarm nodded. "In self-defense," he told her.

"Drop your gunbelt!" the girl demanded, taking a step closer and lifting both barrels. "Unbuckle it slow, you son of a bitch, or I'll blow a hole in your crotch!"

Bo had called the girl Terry. She looked every inch a Dennim. She was as thin as a reed, but her breasts were full and strained against the pale shift of a dress she wore. Her hair, a gleaming tangle of dark tresses, spilled down onto her shoulders. Blue eyes snapped angrily from beneath handsome, broad eyebrows. At the moment her full, passionate mouth was a cold, ruthless line of resolve.

Slowly, carefully, Longarm unbuckled his gunbelt and let it slip to the ground.

"Son of a bitch!" Bo cried, delighted, stepping out of the barn doorway. "The bastard walked right into our hands. Wait'll we tell Will he was out here all along!"

"You are one big fool, mister," the girl told him, slipping the safety off the Greener. "We are going to blow you to hell! What do you think of that?"

Longarm did not think much of it, but before he could reply, the farmhouse door opened and a huge bear of a man strode out onto the porch. At once Bo and Terry turned to look at him. Bo's eyes lit eagerly, and the tip of his tongue poked out to moisten his upper lip. He seemed more than willing to let his father handle matters from here on.

Pa Dennim wore a large black floppy-brimmed hat, bib overalls over a red undershirt, and high, scuffed boots. He had enormous shoulders and a stomach to match. His face was round and beefy, framed with light reddish hair and thick, bushy brows. His eyes were light brown, almost golden. His sandy beard was neatly clipped.

Despite his heft, as he stepped down off the porch and strode toward them, his movements were light, almost graceful. Pulling up a few feet from Longarm, he peered with a fearful wariness at him, his head tipped slightly.

"You the one killed my boy Hank?"

Longarm nodded.

"What fool notion brought you out here?" he demanded.

"I have something to tell you."

Dennim straightened up slightly and took a deep breath. His ruddy face lost its color. Big though the man was, in that instant he seemed to shrink slightly.

"Is it about Will?" he demanded.

Longarm nodded.

A bleak, despairing look came into his eyes. "He's been hurt?"

"He's been killed—shot dead last night."

"You?"

"Yes."

Dennim staggered back as if Longarm had struck him. Then he closed both eyes tightly, his mouth twisting silently as a deep, barely audible groan escaped from him. "Will, oh, Will!" he cried softly. "Will!"

Bo ran quickly, furiously, closer to Longarm and flung up his rifle. "Let me kill him, Pa! Let me!"

"Stand aside, Pa," Terry cried fiercely, moving around her father's bulk, her face dark with fury. "I'll blow the son of a bitch in two!"

"No!" Dennim cried. "No!"

He fixed each of them with a harsh, resolute stare until both lowered their weapons.

Then Dennim looked back at Longarm. "You killed two of my boys. And now you just ride out here to tell me about it? You rode to your damnation just so's you could brag?"

"I didn't come to brag, Dennim."

"Then why?"

"Because I want it to end here. Yes, I killed both of your boys, but neither one gave me any choice. Last night Will fired at me from an alley without warning. What else could I do but return his fire?"

"Did you have to kill him?"

"It was dark. I fired quickly."

"And Hank?"

"Ask Bo. Hank went for his iron when I tried to stop the holdup. Again, Dennim, I had no choice!"

Dennim squinted his eyes shut as he bottled his fury and frustration. It was obvious he knew his sons well enough to realize that Longarm spoke the truth. But this did not make his loss any easier to bear. Nor did it dull in any way the awful pain he felt at that moment.

When he again regarded Longarm, tears coursed

down his cheek. "Fools!" he muttered. "Fools! Both of them! I told them! My God, I told them!"

Then he turned on Bo and Terry. "Put away them weapons!" he cried. "This man is our guest. He told us the truth. Only an honest man would ride in here and dare to tell a man he has killed his two sons."

"Pa!" Bo insisted. "We got to kill him now for what he done!"

"What's the matter with you, boy? You hard of hearin'? It's ending here. Now!"

"But I can kill him right this minute!"

"'Course you can! Don't take any backbone to throw down on an unarmed man! But that ain't the way I raised you, boy! Look at you! Slaverin' to shoot down an unarmed man!"

"But, Pa . . . !" Bo was so frustrated he looked almost ready to cry. "Just let me fix him some! Please, Pa! Please . . . !"

"Don't beg, boy! I swear, you make me sick to look at you. This is what you and them brothers of yours get for goin' agin me and takin' after that stage!"

Dennim strode over to Bo and snatched the rifle from his hand. Then he struck Bo's face with the back of his hand. Bo rocked back, flinging his hand up to his reddening cheek. Like a cowed dog, he backed away from his father.

"Now go get Randy and Clem," Dennim ordered his son. "They're huntin' strays in the north pasture. Then take the flatbed into Snake Flat. Get Will's body. And hurry up—before Will's body gets too rank for a decent burial."

"But, Pa . . . !" Bo cried, still unwilling to believe

his father was not going to move on Longarm. "You ain't going to let this feller go, are you?"

"Damn you, boy!" Dennim thundered. "When I speak, move!"

Grabbing his son cruelly by the arm, he hauled him roughly toward the barn. As Dennim dragged him along, he kept his face close to his boy's as he told him forcefully why he had to obey. Longarm heard nothing of what was said, but apparently it mollified Bo. Pulling away from his father, Bo turned and hurried into the barn to saddle up a horse.

Dennim walked back to his daughter. "Terry," he told her, "I want you to go on inside now and tell your mother about Will. Then tell her we'll be havin' a guest for dinner."

"You mean he's goin' to sit and eat at our table?"

"Damn it, girl! Can't you hear right?"

Terry's face had gone deathly white. She looked in dismay at her father, then swung her glance back to Longarm. For an instant Longarm thought she just might haul up her shotgun and blow him away in blind defiance of her father.

"Put down that shotgun, girl!" Dennim thundered.

Hesitating only a moment longer, she lowered the shotgun, whirled about, and strode angrily toward the house.

Watching the girl disappear into the house, Longarm was as puzzled as were Bo and his sister at Dennim's macabre willingness to offer hospitality to the man who had killed two of his sons.

"There isn't any need for you to invite me in, Dennim," Longarm told the man. "I'd just as soon ride out now. Seems to me it would be pretty hard on you and your missus to have me as a guest."

"It'll be hard, all right," Dennim agreed grudgingly. "But I'd be much obliged, Long, if you'd stay here until Bo gets back with Will's body."

"Why's that?"

Dennim bent down and picked up Longarm's gunbelt. Then he smiled at Longarm. It was a bleak smile. "I just want to make sure Will wasn't backshot, that's all."

Longarm was no longer puzzled.

It was not long before Bo brought the two ranch hands back to the compound at a hard gallop. Dennim had a team already hitched up to the flatbed and waiting. An hour or so before sundown the three started for Snake Flat, the two hands driving the flatbed, Bo astride his mount alongside.

Only then did Dennim invite Longarm into the house for the meal. Entering the large, roughly finished kitchen ahead of him, Dennim introduced Longarm to his wife, Kate. The older woman's eyes were swollen from crying, but she was coldly polite and simply nodded curtly to him after the introduction. Though smaller than her husband by a foot, she was almost as big around. Her gleaming dark hair flowed back over her ample shoulders, reaching as far as her waist. Her eyes, small and black, resembled raisins set in fresh bread dough. As she placed the generously heaped platters down on the table, the tiny cupid's bow of her lips remained set in a firm, determined line.

They ate at a large deal table in the center of the kitchen. No one said grace, and for that Longarm was grateful.

The meal was a hearty one, built around a great slab of steak sliced into quarters. There were heaping side dishes of home fries and steaming turnips. The bread was fresh from the oven and cut into thick slices, with lard for butter, and a great steaming kettle of coffee. Nothing fancy, but the fare was solid and filling. Unfortunately, Longarm ate with a heavy knot in the pit of his stomach, and he was certain the others were experiencing the same difficulty.

There was no conversation. As soon as the meal was finished, Pa Dennim showed Longarm the small upstairs room that would be his while he remained as a guest of the Lazy D. There was a single window hung with clean, roughly sewn potato sacks for curtains, a brass bed with an Indian blanket as a coverlet, a washstand and commode.

"That was Hank's room," Dennim remarked as he closed the door on it.

Then he led the way back down the narrow steps to the first floor and out onto the porch, where the two men sat down to watch the fireflies. Longarm offered Pa Dennim a cheroot. The man took it eagerly and lit up. They smoked for a long while in heavy silence, both aware of the clatter of dishes coming from the kitchen as Dennim's wife and daughter cleaned up.

At last, Longarm bid good night to Dennim, mounted the narrow stairs, and let himself into the dead man's room.

• • •

Longarm came awake in an instant. Slowly, stealthily he closed his hand around the derringer he had taken from his boot earlier and placed under his pillow. Someone had just stolen through the door. What had awakened him was the creak of the hinge. What he heard now were light footfalls approaching his bed.

He was about to swing around suddenly, his derringer blazing, when a deft hand lifted his blanket and he felt a small, lithe body snuggle eagerly up against his long frame. Startled, Longarm was not entirely certain what to do next. Would he be needing the derringer? Then he heard a soft giggle and felt Terry's light finger tracing a path over his face before coming to a halt on his mouth.

Pressing it gently, she said, "Shhh! We must be quiet."

Longarm let go of the derringer and turned slowly to face her. In the darkness he could barely make out her face. She snuggled nearer to him, her arms snaking about his neck, pulling him still closer.

"This don't make any kind of sense, Terry," Longarm said. "Haven't you forgotten something? I killed your brothers."

"Tomorrow, perhaps, we will kill you. But now you are a man. A nice big one. I have not had a man in a long time. Besides, Pa wants us to be hospitable."

"This hospitable?"

"He didn't say. Be quiet."

Longarm pulled back to make room on the bed. As he did so, she stayed with him, flattening her warm body eagerly against his. Gently but firmly, she pushed against his shoulders until he was on his back. Then she kissed him passionately, her full lips devouring his, her tongue thrusting eagerly, probing deeply with delicious, wanton abandon. And all the while, her hot little hands were busy, moving with an expert precision that traced a light, maddening line down his chest, all the way to his crotch.

He felt her body tremble with silent laughter when he responded to her practiced fondling of his fully aroused manhood. She pulled her hand away teasingly while she probed still deeper with her tongue. Then her hand was grabbing at him again, her hand like a scorching flame. He could barely lie still under her maddening caresses. Her lips kept his parted.

Deep, satisfying grunts came from his throat. She pulled her mouth off his and then she darted forward, her teeth nibbling on his upper lip. Teasing, she began sucking it greedily. Abruptly, she fastened her lips about one of his nipples, then moved down his chest to his belly and then his crotch. He groaned aloud as her tongue Frenched him, setting his loins ablaze.

"Shhh!" she whispered fiercely, her face suddenly inches from his. "We must be quiet."

She laughed softly then and began nibbling one of his earlobes.

"Mmmm," she murmured. "There is so *much* of you to play with!"

Longarm grabbed her small, bony buttocks in his big hands and hauled her in under him.

"No!" she hissed. "No! Not that way! I want to ride you!"

She pulled herself away with an urgency that did

not allow Longarm to foil her, then swiftly flung one of her legs across his waist and boosted herself up onto him. With an intent grunt, she planted herself firmly down upon his erection. He felt her sucking him in, pulling him deep. She proceeded to ride him with a furious, ecstatic abandon, her head flung back, the dark mop of her hair exploding out behind her.

Tightening his buttocks, Longarm drove up to meet each thrust as she ground her pubic bone hard against his. Her teeth clenched. The only sound that escaped her now was a kind of mewing groan. She began twisting her head from side to side in time with each shuddering thrust. He ran his hands up and down her spine, feeling the lovely softness of her smooth skin, the straining, rippling muscles.

To his surprise, he found himself growing still larger within her. He grabbed her small, lean buttocks and started slamming her down onto him, meeting each of her downstrokes with a mounting, joyous rush of pleasure. She was still going strong, and she was good, so very damn good! There was no more deliberation now. He had bought his ticket and found a seat, and the train was moving. He became totally lost in the mounting wonder of it. And then he was there! With a sudden, blinding, obliterating rush, the orgasm came. Only dimly was he aware of Terry's mischievous chuckle as he lifted his buttocks high off the bed, sweeping her up with him almost to the ceiling.

At last, the orgasm having washed him clean, he relaxed beneath her, aware of the blood still pounding in his temples. But now it was her turn. She was still bucking doggedly, still clinging to him. A series of short, sharp grunts told him she was getting closer. He reached up and grabbed her thigh bones, then slammed her down hard onto him. She gasped and shuddered from head to toe. A series of rapid contractions followed. Her eyes closed, she groaned softly and kept on bucking loosely. Finally, her eyes shut, panting with her mouth half open, she fell forward onto his broad chest, resting her cheek on the thick mat of hair coiled there.

For a long while they remained in each other's arms, panting softly, letting the world spin past them, his erection still snuggled deep inside her. After a while, sighing softly, she began to kiss him on the lips with a violent, sweaty, passionate intensity. To his astonishment and delight, he felt his erection come alive within her. He threw his arms around her neck and began to thrust.

"Again!" she told him. "I want you again!"

"Shut up and hang on."

She laughed and sat up boldly, her back arching, her breasts rising. He reached up and grabbed them fiercely, his big thumbs grinding against her nipples. There was no finesse now, only a mindless, withering need. Almost grimly they set about establishing a steady, effective rhythm, thrusting and lunging, slamming and battering against each other with a violence he could no longer control. All Longarm knew for sure was that he was still in her. Dimly he heard her grunting and thrusting, her tiny fists beating at him furiously.

And then Terry was coming in a steady stream of

involuntary, pulsing contractions that seemed to suck him even more deeply inside her. A second later he too exploded, grabbing her fiercely as he emptied himself deep inside of her. For a moment the two clung to each other. And then at last the storm passed. They grew quiet as she collapsed forward onto him, her flushed, drenched face resting on his chest.

"Ummm!" she murmured. "I just couldn't stop. You set me off like a string of firecrackers!"

He chuckled and rolled her over to his side and brushed her dark hair back lightly, aware of the fine beads of moisture that covered her face. Then he petted her trembling, nude flanks and pulled her gently against him again, aware of a surprising, unnerving gentleness.

"You are still my enemy!" she told him fiercely. "I want to kill you! But I knew you'd be this good the minute I laid eyes on you. I just knew it."

Her words chilled him. As words of endearment, they left something to be desired. He had never felt this much hatred in a woman—or this much passion. She was a contradiction that caused a shudder to pass up his spine.

"Maybe you better leave now," he told her.

At his words, she stiffened. He felt her shrinking in his arms, growing perceptibly colder. Gently he pushed her from him.

"Yes," she said. "I got what I wanted. Thank you, Mr. Long."

She pushed herself back off the bed and stood up. He watched her pale figure in the darkness. She had stepped out of her nightgown an instant before slipping into the bed beside him. It lay in a puddle of moonlight on the floor.

He watched her bend to pick up the nightgown. She straightened and ducked her head into it. Shimmering, the nightgown cascaded down over her slim figure. Her head, dark with curls, emerged from the neck, then her arms through the sleeves. She smiled and took a step toward him. He expected her to lean her face close for one last kiss. Instead, she lifted her right hand.

A long knife blade gleamed in the moonlight.

With a sibilant hiss, Terry brought the blade down. As it flashed toward him, Longarm barely managed to ward it off with an upraised forearm. The blade sliced into his flesh, then glanced off the bone. Again the knife slashed down. Unwilling to use his derringer, Longarm snatched up a pillow and warded off her second lunging slash. The knife sliced through the pillow casing, releasing a cloud of feathers.

Behind Terry the door slammed open. Dennim stood in the doorway, a guttering kerosene lamp in his hand.

"Terry!"

The voice of her father halted Terry in the midst of a downstroke. Leaping from the bed, Longarm grabbed her wrist and twisted. With a tiny cry, Terry let the knife clatter to the floor.

Chapter 6

Dennim strode angrily into the room, grabbed his daughter by the arm, and spun her around to face him.

"What in tarnation you doin' in here, girl?"

"She tried to use me for a pincushion," Longarm drawled.

He lit the lamp on the wash stand, then handed Dennim the large bread knife Terry had brought into his room with her. The way he figured it, as she stepped out of her nightgown, she must have dropped the knife onto it. When she slipped back into the gown, she just picked up the knife.

Dennim shook the knife in Terry's face. "You try to use this on our guest, did you?"

"Yes," she snapped defiantly.

Dennim slapped Terry hard.

"Get back to your room!" he told her. "I'll tend to you tomorrow!"

As Terry fled from the room, Dennim looked back at Longarm, his eyes on Longarm's bloody forearm.

"You hurt bad?"

"No. She just caught me on the arm here. It's bleedin' some, but it's only a flesh wound."

"I'll get my woman. She'll put a bandage on it. Don't want you to ruin her bedsheets."

A moment later Dennim's wife entered and silently but efficiently washed the laceration, then bound it tightly with torn strips of fresh linen, after which she pulled the bedsheets off the mattress, leaving Longarm with only the Indian blanket for covers.

As Dennim pulled the door shut after her, he paused in the open doorway and glanced back at Longarm. "Maybe you better move that commode over in front of the door. I don't trust Terry. She's liable to try again." Dennim grinned proudly. "She's a real chip off the old block, that one."

He pulled the door shut. Longarm walked over to the commode and began to drag it over to the door.

It was mid-afternoon the next day. That morning he had heard Dennim going at Terry with a strap. To her credit, the girl had not cried out once during the fierce strapping, and whenever Longarm met her gaze afterward, her return look was proudly defiant.

Now, sitting beside a taciturn Dennim and smoking his last cheroot, Longarm watched as the returning flatbed approached the ranch. Bo and the two ranch hands must have ridden through the night without pause, then turned right around when they secured Will's corpse. Bo Dennim and Clem were riding alongside the wagon. It was probably Will's horse Clem was riding. The other ranch hand, Randy, was driving the flatbed.

Dennim had already strapped a sidearm to his thigh and Longarm's black was saddled and waiting at the hitch rail in front of the ranch house, his gunbelt slung over the saddle. Soon Longarm would be on his way. All that remained now was for Dennim to inspect his son's corpse to make sure that Longarm had told the truth—that he had not shot Will from behind.

It did not matter, apparently, that Will Dennim had been perfectly willing to backshoot Longarm.

As the flatbed neared the ranch house, Dennim got to his feet, visibly braced himself for the ordeal ahead of him, then descended the veranda steps. Longarm accompanied him, his right hand dropping idly into the side pocket of his buckskin jacket, where he had stashed his derringer. Behind him, Longarm heard the door to the house open. He glanced back. Terry and her mother were stepping out onto the veranda to watch.

Randy pulled the team to a halt, then wrapped the reins about the brake handle and quickly boosted himself down off the seat, his eyes averted. Clem seemed just as anxious as his partner to get away from the flatbed as he dismounted and led his horse quickly away from the wagon toward the barn.

Longarm closed his right fist about the derringer.

Bo Dennim spurred closer, his face a grim mask. Reining his mount to a halt in front of his father, he dismounted and stalked angrily up to him.

"Take a look, Pa!" he snapped coldly. "Go see what that son of a bitch did to Will!"

Angrily, Dennim strode around to the bed of the wagon and peered over the side. Keeping close beside him, Longarm did the same. What he saw appalled him. Will's corpse was lying face down on a yellow slicker, with three neat bullet holes in his back.

"Backshot!" Dennim cried, turning on Longarm, his hand clawing for his sixgun.

But Longarm's derringer was already leaping from his side pocket. Pressing the derringer's twin barrels into the flesh under Dennim's chin, Longarm swiftly disarmed Dennim. Then he flung the man brutally back against Bo, who was already drawing his own sixgun. Stepping swiftly close, Longarm cracked Bo on the side of the head with his father's Colt. Bo managed to stay on his feet as Longarm disarmed him and flung his gun across the yard. The two ranch hands were now bolting for the cover of the barn.

Covering Bo and Dennim, Longarm chanced a quick glance back at the house. Ma Dennim was still on the veranda, but Terry had disappeared back inside. In a moment, Longarm knew, Terry would reappear on the porch with that Greener.

He raced to his horse, mounted up—grabbing his gunbelt off the saddle as he did so—then lifted the black to a swift gallop. As he raced away from the house, he glanced back and saw Terry bolt out of the house with the shotgun. He ducked low and roweled the black furiously. Above the pounding of its hooves, he heard the Greener's thunderous detonation. A second later he felt the hot wind of buckshot passing close over his head. The spread was just enough to tick his hat forward.

A moment later he was out of range, galloping hard for the distant saw-toothed peaks that rimmed the valley.

Longarm had a quarter-mile lead on his pursuers. The pound of their horses' hoofs drummed steadily in his ears, but in less than an hour he was sure he had increased his lead. One horse and rider made better time than a crowd.

He stayed with a thin, barely perceptible trace that took him over a saddle and across a small, narrow meadow. The trace continued on into the foothills, but he left it and wheeled into a patch of timber just above the meadow, and kept in it as he cut back parallel with the meadow until he reached its farthest end. Here, sheltered high in the pines, he gave his horse a chance to blow and peered down through the trees at the open land over which he had just ridden.

Bo broke into view first, Dennim pounding along beside him, Terry a few lengths behind them. The two ranch hands were strung out behind her. All of them were punishing their horses something fierce. As Dennim rode, he was pointing to Longarm's tracks as they followed the trace across the meadow. In a moment the five riders swept out of Longarm's line of sight.

The timber around Longarm was old first-growth pine, massive at the butt and rising in flawless line toward a mass of top covering, which made a solid umbrella against sunlight. There was little underbrush and at certain angles he was able to peer for a hundred or two hundred yards through the timber. The sound of his pursuers faded gradually until the silence of the hills lay over everything—until even the breathing of his black seemed disturbingly loud.

It would not be long, Longarm realized, before the Dennims would discover his maneuver. They would backtrack then and find his solitary set of tracks on the spongy humus. But this would not be for a little while. Longarm figured he had time enough now to reach the foothills and the peaks beyond. Once he had given the Dennims the slip entirely, he would seek out Dan Saxon's ranch and see if Rita Saxon's offer was still good. It might be a smart idea to have a few riders at his back the next time he met the Dennims.

No matter what he had been able to do, it seemed, he was finding himself lining up against Jake Telford.

He cut up through the timber, heading for high country. The red-barked trees ran solemnly before him, and somewhere high above the arch of boughs, the afternoon sun blazed. But here the air was shadowed and still and fragrant with the smell of pine and wildflowers. He came presently upon the relic of an ancient wagon road, its twin ruts wiggling before him. Later he came upon the caved-in wreckage of a log-and-shake cabin.

Almost imperceptibly, the country roughened and the pines were smaller. The ravines began to come down toward him. He held to the crest of the ridges as long as possible, then dropped into a ravine, crossed over a shallow stream, and found himself entering a wide canyon. He pulled up. It felt too much like a trap to him, and he decided to climb out of it. Spotting a game trail to his left, he followed it across a talus-littered slope and found a steep-sided gully beyond it that led up through the canyon's folds. Keeping to the gully, Longarm found himself at last nearing the rim of the canyon, and a thick stand of timber beyond.

Once in the timber, he felt considerably better. He rode steadily higher, his horse's hoofs biting silently into the pine needles that carpeted the timberland. An hour or so before sunset the trees ahead of him thinned, and he glimpsed through them a creek rushing over a shallow, immaculate bed of gravel. Beyond the creek the heavy timber took over once more and continued its march up the mountainside.

Pulling up, Longarm sat his mount quietly, patting the black's neck to keep it quiet. For at least five minutes he stayed within the timber, peering warily out at the lower and upper reaches of the creek and at the timber on the far side. At last, satisfied that he was alone, he nudged the black out of the timber and rode to the water's edge. He let the horse slake its thirst, then forded the stream. Twenty yards inside the timber on the other side, he came to a trail looping stiffly up the side of the mountain. He decided to follow it.

He rose with the short switchback courses, moving higher and higher along the edge of the cliff. He arrived at last at a level stretch of meadow that clung precariously to the side of the mountain, gave the trail below him one last glance, then rode still higher. He found a ridge, kept moving along its spine, came to another ridge, and was soon high above the small meadow he had so recently left.

He kept on until the trail he was following brought him to a complete standstill at the edge of a precipice. He peered cautiously over the black's neck. The gorge was at least a three-hundred-foot drop into the black bowels of another canyon.

Longarm cursed silently and looked about him. The land was deceptive. He had ridden out of one canyon to this height, and now he found himself facing another canyon—only this time he was trapped on a kind of island, afloat in a dizzying emptiness. He had less than an hour's light left in the sky. Already a cool wind was blowing off the peaks above him. Longarm peered down into the canyon and saw the tide of blackness slowly filling the canyon.

Ahead of him, all he could make out was a narrow game trail that dropped along the face of the gorge at a dangerously steep angle. His eye followed its thin tracery until it vanished into the darkness below him. Longarm judged it had not been used recently and was no more than a path cut out by deer and other sure-footed mountain creatures.

There had to be a better way of moving off this ridge. One end of the ridge had to be anchored against the mountainside, and that would certainly provide him with a level enough route. But that would mean going back. And there was no assurance that he would find it before night fell. With a troubled sigh, he put the horse onto the game trail and began to follow the trail into the gorge.

The cliffside was rock and earth, with some vegetation clinging to it. The trail itself was no more than four or five feet wide, sometimes hugging the cliff so closely that his leg rubbed sharply against the rough outcropping of rock. The black was both tired and doubtful. It stopped frequently and had to be pressed on by Longarm's spurs. At some places, the trail pitched forward so steeply that the horse's front feet slid along the loose rubble.

Soon, dusk fell over him like a clammy blanket. He glanced up. The light was draining rapidly from the sky. He might as well have been at the bottom of a well. He kept going, nevertheless. Night fell like a black, seamless cloak, sucking up every particle of light. He hoped for a moon, but it was too early. Before long, the darkness was complete—an unnerving, smothering limbo. And what made it even more difficult was the lack of visual reference points he needed to help him keep his balance in the saddle.

Doggedly, he urged the black on.

The horse kept on famously for a while. Then, without warning, it stopped, refusing to move an inch farther down the trail. Longarm urged it on for a moment or two, then bent forward in the saddle and fixed his eyes upon a spot where he expected the trail ahead of him to be. Before long he thought he caught a dim intimation of the trail moving straight ahead through the blackness before him.

Again he urged the horse on, more insistently this time. Instead of going forward, however, the black gathered its feet close together and began to turn about on the narrow trail, gingerly and slowly, in little mincing steps, until it had reversed itself completely. Then, pointing downward still, it moved on. Glancing back over his shoulder, Longarm this time saw the drop-off where the trail had switched back.

Longarm had tried to get the black to step out into space.

When he realized how badly his eyes had failed him, Longarm felt more than a twinge of uncertainty. He was now less than halfway down a cliff whose total drop was something like three hundred feet. He grew anxious to have this excruciating passage done with, but he let the reins remain slack, convinced now that his best bet was to trust to the black.

The next time the horse pulled up, Longarm made no effort to keep it going. He bent forward in the saddle. Again he saw nothing. He waited for the horse to move. He waited a full two to three minutes, then slid carefully to the ground and moved forward, crowding himself carefully between the canyon wall and the black. Once in front of the horse, he got down on his hands and knees and used his hands to feel the trail ahead of him.

A rock slide blocked the trail entirely. Longarm stood up, running his arm forward, trying to feel out the depth of the barrier. It was a new slide, the dirt not yet packed firmly, and it did not appear to be very wide. He ran his hands into the dirt and found he could move it. Crouching, he began throwing the loose dirt and rocks off the trail into the abyss below him. He heard the rocks strike the canyon floor long after he had let them fly, and was able to judge roughly how high they were still.

It took him better than half an hour to clear a

pathway through the barrier. Catching up the black's reins with his bruised and raw fingers, he led the horse cautiously forward. Fifty feet brought him to an uncertain spot and he stopped once more and dropped again to his hands and knees. This time he discovered he had come to another switchback. He let the horse take its time making its swing, and kept going.

There was a swift stream flowing at the bottom of the canyon. Its cold dampness rose to meet him as the sound of it grew steadily louder. Longarm had begun this descent an hour before, perhaps even two, and he felt the strain of it. But he kept going doggedly, walking with a short forward step. He was as cautious as ever, but he was beginning to think the worst was over as the bottom of floor of the canyon came closer— as evidenced by the growing clamor of the stream.

He took a step—and found no trail to meet his foot. He lost his balance and dropped forward into emptiness.

He had been holding the black's reins tightly. Now he grasped them more firmly as he was flung forward, one foot still on the trail. The weight of his body pulled suddenly on the horse, but the reins held. The black took the sudden pressure with a startled upward fling of its head, hauling Longarm upward. Longarm whipped himself around, grasped the reins with both hands, and swung outward into space. As he slammed back against the cliffside, he tried to find a toehold with his boots. But he found no foothold and continued to drop until his chest slammed down heavily onto a sharp outcropping of rock.

Alarmed, the horse moved backward, this action

only aggravating Longarm's predicament as his ribs were dragged cruelly up over the edge of the outcropping. Despite this, Longarm managed to get one elbow hooked over the rocks. He was then able to let the reins go and anchor himself with both elbows. For a long moment he hung there, regaining his breath, the toes of his boots digging hopefully at the steep slope, seeking a foothold, any kind of foothold. At last he found a place to lodge one toe. Lifting himself gently, his elbows taking most of his weight, he pushed himself upward and managed finally to crawl back up onto the trail. Rolling over, he sat upright.

After a long while, he got back up onto his feet. He couldn't see the horse, but he could smell it close beside him. With groping hands he found its muzzle and pulled the horse closer, patting it thankfully on the neck. Then he walked back to the break in the trail, shuffling his feet until he reached the break. He got down on his hands and knees and reached out. He found nothing. Nothing at all. Only a cold wind that blew up from the inky darkness below.

He sat back a moment, drawing a long breath. Then he flattened himself on his belly and inched forward until he teetered on the edge of the break like a balanced board and reached out again. For the second time he touched nothing. That meant the gap was wider than three feet.

He found a couple of small rocks on the trail and threw one of them a distance he judged to be more than three feet. It fell short. He threw the second one a farther distance and heard it land on the trail. That made the gap somewhere between five and eight feet.

He sat back, defeated and exasperated. He tried to visualize the break and couldn't. Then he took out his tin of sulfur matches and struck one. What he saw startled him. Just before the gap, the trail ducked sharply to the right, into a cleft in the side of the mountain, reappearing on other side of the gap. The trail that followed into the cleft was only half the width of the original trail; but there was enough room on it for both him and the horse if they inched along it single file and hugged the cliff wall.

The match guttered out.

Longarm got back up, went back for the horse, and took its reins. Then, speaking to it softly, soothingly, led it forward. The horse was a sure-footed brute, made wary by his experiences of the last hour— and when he came to the spot where Longarm had almost stepped into perdition, he hauled back on the reins and planted both front feet solidly on the ground.

Longarm turned and leaned his cheek close to the black's.

"Easy does it, boy. You got to keep going now. Just stay close behind me."

The horse was trembling. Longarm did not force the issue. He waited patiently until the horse calmed down somewhat. Then he started up again, pulling gently, talking soothingly to the horse all the while. A few loose stones were kicked free and went flying off into the blackness, but Longarm hugged the wall as he followed the trail into the cleft, moving at a steady but achingly slow pace.

At last Longarm was beyond the dip in the cliffside, and a moment later he felt the solid ground beneath his feet. Turning, he pulled the horse after him. The horse lunged suddenly and joined Longarm on the wider, more solid portion of the trail. The horse seemed as pleased as Longarm. Nickering softly, the black nuzzled Longarm's neck. Longarm grinned and kept going, leading the horse steadily downward, taking his steps with infinite caution, aware by this time that he was very tired. The rush of the river below him was growing louder by the minute, reminding Longarm how good a drink of that ice-cold water would taste.

They reached the canyon floor at last, the trail playing out through gravel and great chunks of rock at the river's edge. The gravel churned under Longarm's boots. The black stumbled and pulled up. Longarm understood. The animal was dead beat. Longarm pulled it on until they came to better footing. Then he unsaddled the horse, put hobbles on it, and together they slaked their thirst in the stream.

Then Longarm made his camp, rolled up in his soogan, and slept.

Chapter 7

What awoke Longarm around midnight was something hard burrowing into his back. He sat, reached back, and flung the stone away. He tried to find a better spot for his bedroll, but he awoke again to find other stones growing under him. He rose wearily and carried his bedroll to higher ground, above the gravel bed flanking the stream. The rest of the night he slept fitfully, and he awoke at last in time to see the first faint streaks of light seeping into the sky above the canyon's distant rim.

He saddled up and rode the length of the canyon, keeping to the gravel bordering the stream. Soon he had left the rough country behind as he climbed still higher into the mountains. By noon he was moving freely over lush parklands, riding toward those twin peaks Rita Saxon had pointed out to him.

By late afternoon, the black was almost played out, and the twin peaks were dominating the sky ahead of him; but still he had not reached the Saxon spread. He came to a stream, watered his horse, and decided to camp early. Remembering his ordeal of the night before, he followed the stream into the timber. Once in the pines, he saw through the trees ahead of him a narrow stretch of meadowland, on the far edge of which there appeared to be the remains of a ranch building.

He kept on through the timber and crossed the stream-bordered meadow. There was a wooded bluff at the far end, the crumbling ranch building sitting just below it. As soon as Longarm was close enough, he could see that it was the remains of a bunkhouse. Riding up to it, he saw further on, closer to the bluff, the burnt-out remains of a ranch house and barn, the weathered stumps of an old corral poking up through the high grass.

Dismounting, Longarm stepped through the bunk-house doorway. It was a long, fairly well constructed building that extended some distance toward the bluff. He saw the remains of bunk frames around the walls, and a doorway that led into a much longer room beyond. A huge black stove crouched at the far end.

He was about to step back out of the building when he heard a clear, distinct shout—and recognized Dennim's hoarse voice.

"We been waitin' for you, Long!"

Glancing out through the doorway, he saw Dennim

standing on the edge of the bluff, at least four hundred feet away. The man brought up his rifle and fired, the bullet thudding into the side of the bunkhouse a few feet from him.

The black was twenty feet from the doorway, flinging up his head at the sound of the rifle shot. Longarm ducked out, grabbed the horse's reins, and led it back toward the building. A bullet broke the ground ahead of him and another one splintered the side of the bunkhouse as he jumped through the doorway, pulling the horse in after him.

As Longarm led the horse deeper into the building, Dennim began pumping shots methodically down onto the shack. He laid a pattern around the outside edge of the door, then began firing through the roof. Lead came crashing through the shakes with small, gusty snorts. Longarm backed away, watching the wood splinters spring up into the air as the lead pounded into the floorboards. The bullet holes were marching steadily toward him. He caught the black's bridle and moved through the inner doorway, all the way back to the big stove. The bullets followed after him. Soon the interior of the place was thick with the dusty residue of the shattered shakes and exploded wood.

There was another door in this room across from the stove. It opened out onto the meadow. But it was much closer to the bluff than the other entrance.

The firing ceased for a moment. Dennim was probably taking time out to reload, or perhaps to improve his position. Longarm knew that if he stayed inside the bunkhouse a chance shot would sooner or later reach him or cripple the black. He noticed, from the pattern of bullet holes on the floor, that Dennim had set about his task with a design—to cover the bunkhouse from one end to the other. He had already reached to within fifteen feet of where Longarm stood.

He stepped to a side window and looked out. He could no longer see Dennim on the bluff. He walked to the door, took off his hat, and peered carefully out. Dennim was still up on the bluff, but he had just moved along it to a spot that brought him at least twenty yards closer. Beside him stood Bo, Terry, and the two ranch hands. All of them carried rifles and were poised to fire at the first good target.

Longarm stepped out from the doorway and let them see him. Before they could fire at him, he ducked back into the bunkhouse. Unlimbering his rifle, he broke out the remaining window panes and fired up at the bluff. At once a fusillade answered. As the bullets crashed into the bunkhouse, Longarm led his horse back the full length of the bunkhouse and stood before the other door. The bullets continued to crash down onto the bunkhouse, the fire now concentrating on the other portion of the bunkhouse. A few rounds ricocheted off the stove.

Longarm caught the black's reins in his left hand, slapped the horse out through the open doorway, then vaulted into the saddle. He was already twenty feet from the bunkhouse, loping down the meadow parallel to the stream, when Dennim's party swung their rifles over and began to reach out for him. He kept going, heading for cover under the bluff. Veering in closer to it, he scraped the edge of the bluff and, looking back, saw Bo leaning out over the rim, trying to land an accurate shot. His bullet missed by three or four feet, digging at the soft ground before him. Longarm turned with the bluff's gradual bend and when he looked back up at the ridge again he found himself sheltered by the bluff's pine-crowded overhang.

Pulling up, he studied his situation. The bluff's slope was too sheer for him to climb, and not ten feet from him the stream had cut a narrow swath through the high, soft meadow. Beyond the stream the rough shoulders of a ridge came down in heavy folds of timber and rock. It was a rough slope, but a passable one, once he crossed the stream.

The stream itself, freshly born in these hills, was small and shallow and fast. He put his horse over the meadow and into the water. At once he heard the renewal of gunfire as he moved out into the stream, away from the protective wing of the bluff's overhang. Pointing the black upstream for better footing, he felt the current break hard against the horse's legs. At the halfway point the water began to push against the black's barrel and chest—and a bullet struck the surface of the stream close by. Struggling with the slippery rocks, the black came to a full pause to gain his balance, then moved on, working steadily through the shallows. Beyond a narrow sandbar on the far side loomed a steep-sided bank, timber crowning it. Longarm urged his mount toward it. The horse dug valiantly up the embankment and plunged into the timber. Not until they were well into it did Longarm pull up to give the black a chance to blow.

For a moment he thought he caught the hoofbeats of horsemen above him in the timber. He froze, his hand about the black's muzzle as he listened. But all he could hear was the distant sighing of the wind high in the pines. He relaxed and took a drink from his canteen. Then he spurred the horse still deeper into the pines, heading for a red shale limestone ridge he had glimpsed through the trees ahead of him.

He broke from the timber at last and found himself crossing a pine-stippled meadow stretching ahead of him to the base of a timbered slope buttressing the ridge. Urging the black to a hard gallop, he pounded across the meadow and plunged into the timber. Dismounting, he led the horse up the sloping, slippery floor of pine needles. As soon as he reached the ridge, he snaked his rifle from its boot and tethered the black to a pine. Then he moved up onto the ridge. He found a weathered channel that led to its edge and followed it, keeping low. Wedging himself down between two blocks of limestone, he peered across the meadow and waited for his pursuers to show themselves.

They pounded out of the timber in single file. Dennim was in the lead, Bo and Terry trailing, the two ranch hands a good distance back. Those two hands were not, Longarm realized, very enthusiastic about this business.

Longarm cranked a round into the Winchester's firing chamber and lifted the rifle to his shoulder. Making a shrewd guess at the distance, he rested his sights on Dennim, then lifted the muzzle slightly and squeezed the trigger. Longarm missed—as he had intended—but Dennim had felt the bullet's passage. He ducked his head and turned his horse back toward the timber. Bo, however, was not to be so easily intimidated. Leaving his father and Terry behind, he spurred furiously on across the meadow.

With a bitter sigh, Longarm tracked him carefully and fired. The slug caught him high and with the force of a sledgehammer, flinging him violently back off the horse. With a cry, Dennim wheeled and spurred back out onto the meadow to where Bo lay. Longarm cranked a fresh cartridge into the firing chamber and watched gloomily.

Dennim flung himself from his horse and cradled his last son's head in his lap. Terry, seeing that Longarm had not fired on her father, galloped out also. The two ranch hands were still hanging well back, watching from their horses. Terry flung herself from her horse and crouched beside her brother.

Pulling himself up onto one of the limestone blocks so that he was visible to Dennim and Terry, he cranked a fresh round into the Winchester and stood for a moment looking down at them. Terry saw him first. She jumped up and pointed.

"Dennim!" Longarm called down to the man. "I told you the truth! It wasn't me put those bullets in Will's back! Bo did!"

Dennim lurched upright and raised a fist. "That don't make no difference!" the man screamed, his voice coming faint but clear. "Bo's dead! You killed him!"

Snatching up his rifle, Dennim began pouring shots up at the ridge as fast as he could work the lever. As his slugs ricocheted off the rocks, Longarm moved back off the ledge and returned to his black.

Swinging aboard the animal, he rode into the timber and kept going up the slope of the mountain's flank at a steady but unhurried pace. There was no need for him to punish the horse any further. Dennim would be too busy burying his last son to keep after him now. Longarm should have felt some relief at that thought, but he did not.

He had just taken Dennim's last son from him, and sooner or later Longarm would have to answer for that.

The timber gave way to a deeply eroded scar caused by an ancient landslide, and soon Longarm was fighting his way over some of the roughest ground he had ever experienced. He dismounted and began to lead the black, breaking through vine undergrowth, circling great masses of fallen rock and soil, skirting logs lying abreast before him. The horse came patiently after him, occasionally taking a narrow gully with a lunge that pushed Longarm out of the way, sometimes balancing himself on a grade so steep that only Longarm's added weight on the bridle kept the horse from sliding down the slope.

This was the way of it for half an hour. Presently a steep-sided, chute-like ravine in the torn ground led down the slope toward a small glen. Keeping to the ravine, Longarm made better time. And eventually he came out upon an area of bald, worn rock. He passed around several boulders at least two stories high and discovered a trail winding between great curving walls of limestone rock that seemed to have been torn from the depths of the mountain.

He kept going, reached another huge boulder, passed around it, and came out upon a grassy sward. Mounting up, he soon put the mountain's raw, open wound behind him and found himself in timber once again. During all that struggle, a brilliant sunset had gone unnoticed, and now darkness was falling over the timber like a chill cloak.

He was starting to look for a campsite when he saw the gleam of a campfire through the trees. It could well be Circle S ranch hands, he realized. Dismounting, he tethered the black to a sapling and approached cautiously, his Colt out. Once he reached the clearing, he peered through a large fern and was surprised to see a familiar figure carefully settling a coffee pot down into the campfire's hot coals.

It was the bearded fellow the bar girl had called Mike, the one Longarm thought he knew from somewhere else. He was wearing a black, flat-crowned sombrero, a battered sheepskin coat, Levi's, and well-scuffed riding boots.

Longarm stepped into the small clearing.

Mike glanced over and smiled, almost as if he had been expecting Longarm.

"You can put that gun down, Mr. Long," he said. "It won't get this coffee ready any sooner."

Longarm holstered his Colt and walked closer.

Mike got easily to his feet, a huge Colt materializing in his hand, its muzzle aimed at Longarm's head.

121

He had been holding it covertly against the outside of his thigh all the while.

"Okay, Carl!" Mike called.

Longarm heard another man step out of the timber behind him. He glanced over. This one had a rifle in his hand. He was clean-shaven, with a face shaped like a hatchet and eyes that peered venomously at Longarm as he moved up quickly behind Longarm and lifted the Colt from his holster.

"I knew the light from this here campfire would draw him," Carl said, obviously relishing the neatness with which they had closed their trap.

"Like a moth to a flame," agreed Mike.

The man's reddish beard covered the entire lower portion of his face, and he wore his sombrero so far down over his forehead that there was too little of his face visible for Longarm's memory to get a handle on. But it was trying.

Mike glanced at Longarm. "We didn't think you'd ever get over that stretch of badland. We thought we might hurry you along with some nicely placed shots, but we didn't want you to piss your pants."

"Who do you boys ride for?" Longarm asked. "The Circle S?"

"Hell, no," said Mike. He seemed to be enjoying himself. He took out a cigar and lit it. "We're T Bar riders. Jake sent us here to keep a look out for you. We been following you since you hightailed it out of Dennim's spread."

"And you didn't do anything to help them catch me?"

"Nope. We just placed our bets and kept out of the way. They sure as hell are an unlucky tribe, I'd say. It's just Pa and that girl left now. You sure as hell trimmed them down some."

"What's Jake Telford want with me?"

"Jake has a few question he wants to ask."

"About what?"

Mike chuckled. "Why don't you ask *him* that?"

"If it's about my joining with him, you can tell him I'm playing this hand alone."

Carl leaned closer. "Look, mister, you ain't got no more cards to play, the way Mike and me see it. So just relax. You're comin' with us."

"I don't think so."

Carl clubbed Longarm on the side of the head with the barrel of his sixgun. Longarm felt the ground slam up into his back. When he was able to focus his eyes again, he saw Carl smiling down at him. "It don't matter to me none, mister. You can ride in to the T Bar aboard that big black or we can sling you over his pommel. Don't make no never mind to us which way you want it to be."

Longarm shrugged and pushed himself to a sitting position. "All right, then. But let's have some of that coffee first."

"Good idea," said Mike, chuckling.

On their way back to Telford's ranch, Mike and Carl kept to the high ridges and bluffs. They were traversing a long benchland when Longarm saw the lights of a ranch gleaming in the darkness below them. When

123

he inquired, Mike told him it was Saxon's Circle S. The ranch buildings, Longarm noticed, were clustered about the coil of a mountain stream, with steep, timbered hills flanking the compound on three sides.

By the time they reached the T Bar, the moon was high. In the shadow of ragged hills to the west and south, Longarm saw ahead of him a dim confusion of rectangular shapes which gradually materialized into sheds and barns, their roofs pale in the moonlight. Before long, the night wind brought to him the smell of barns and penned livestock. The gleaming black band of a wide creek spilling out of the hills meandered toward them. A plank bridge appeared and they boomed across it. A few minutes later they were pulling up in front of a solid log house built low and long on a slight rise. Massive cottonwoods loomed over the house, their pale leaves whispering in the night wind.

As Longarm dismounted, he saw the ranch house door open. Lamps came on inside the house, turning two of the downstairs windows into yellow rectangles of light. Jake Telford was standing in the doorway, a rifle in his hand.

"I see you got him, Mike," Telford said, obviously pleased.

"That I did, Jake," Mike answered. He had also dismounted and had moved to a spot behind Longarm. "We found him where you said we would. He stung Bo Dennim pretty bad, looks like."

"Nice work, Mike—you too, Carl."

"Here's his gun," Carl said, mounting the steps

and handing it to Telford.

"Up here, Long," Telford said, sticking the sixgun into his belt.

As Longarm mounted the steps, Mike called up to him.

"I guess you don't remember me, do you, Mr. Long?"

Longarm paused and turned. "Should I?"

"I wear this beard as thick as I do for a reason. There's a pretty mean scar runs from my chin all the way up to my cheekbone. Remember now, do you?"

"Hell, no. Why should I?"

"Because you put it there, Longarm. Five years ago."

In that instant Longarm recalled those bright blue eyes and the knife fight in a border cantina. It had been a deadly struggle, one Longarm had not asked for. But he had left his opponent for dead and kept after the two gents Billy had sent him to bring in. Only when Longarm was back in Denver had he learned the identity of the man he thought he had killed. Mike Deaver. He was a member of a gang Wallace had tracked all the way into Canada, then lost.

Now Mike Deaver was smiling up at him, his teeth gleaming in the moonlight. "You was a deputy U. S. marshal then," Mike said. "Some called you Longarm. I came after you that night 'cause I thought you was after me. Who're you after this time, Longarm?"

Mike laughed then and strode off.

Longarm turned to see Jake Telford smiling coldly at him, his rifle aimed at Longarm's belly button.

"Looks like we got some talking to do, Longarm," he said. "Get inside."

Marie, the percentage girl Mike had offered to Longarm at the Bagdad saloon, was sprawled on a leather sofa in the living room, a long cotton nightgown barely covering her charms. Glancing irritably at the girl as he entered, Telford told her curtly to get her ass off the furniture and wait for him upstairs.

As Marie fled the room, Longarm sat down in an upholstered Morris chair while Telford slumped down on the leather sofa. After dumping Longarm's Colt on a battered table in front of the sofa, Telford leaned the rifle he was carrying against the wall and regarded Longarm closely.

"Let's have it," he said. "What're you doin' in Snake Flat? Like Mike said, who're you after?"

"You know what I'm doing here. Like the rest of you, I'm running from the law."

"The great Longarm? How the hell do you expect me to believe that?"

Longarm shrugged. "I took some liberties with government money. Half a shipment of gold I was supposed to bring back after I recovered it found its way into a bank account under my name. I guess I would have been smarter if I'd used an assumed name."

"I don't believe you."

"Why not?"

"Quite a few of my boys have heard of you. So have I, as a matter of fact. And what they know—and what I know—makes us all real unhappy thinkin' of you prowling around. I'll ask you again. Who or what are you after?"

"And I'll tell you. I'm looking for a place to hide."

"It don't sound right."

"It's the truth."

"Lawmen have gone bad before. I've seen it. Hell, there's times I've helped in the process. But not the famous Longarm. Not you."

Longarm sighed. "Try me."

Telford's eyes narrowed. "How do you mean?"

"Didn't you say you wanted my gun on your side against Saxon and the others?"

"That was before I knew who you were."

Longarm smiled. "I can still use a gun. And I'd still like a chance at that ranch you promised me."

"You've changed your tune, ain't you?"

"You heard what Mike told you. I couldn't get Pa Dennim and his son to listen to reason. Bo fixed me good, and not long after that I had to blow the poor son of a bitch out of his saddle. Pa Dennim's going to be coming after me soon, like an unhappy grizzly. So maybe I'll be needing your help."

Telford shook his head. "It just don't sound right. You're a lawman. The stripe's in you too deep to wash out."

"I'm telling you the truth, Telford."

Telford regarded Longarm morosely for a moment, then shook his head. "Hell, this shit could go on all night."

He got to his feet and went to the door. Opening it, he called out the names of two men and returned to the living room. When the two hands tramped into the house a moment later in answer to his summons, Telford indicated Longarm with a weary nod of his head.

"Truss the son of a bitch good and proper and dump him in the back room in the bunkhouse. I got other business waiting for me upstairs right now. We'll find out what he's up to tomorrow."

The two men marched out of the house, Longarm between them. Longarm counted himself lucky that that percentage girl was upstairs waiting for Telford. Now all he hoped for was that these two men would not notice the slight bulge in the back of his right boot as they tied him up for the night.

Chapter 8

As Longarm had hoped, the two men trussed him so hastily and unceremoniously that they did not notice the derringer hidden in his right boot. Nevertheless, so tightly were his wrists and ankles bound together behind his back that he had an almost impossible task working off the boot.

And while he struggled silently in the small utility room, he could not help but overhear what Telford's men relaxing in their bunks in the next room were discussing. Scamper juice was being passed around generously, and the result was loud, boisterous talk. The gist of it was that Telford planned to move soon on Dan Saxon's Circle S before the cattleman could rally to his side those remaining ranchers who had not yet sold out to Telford. Just when the attack would come, Longarm could not be certain. But from the sound of the men's talk, it would come within a day or two.

By the time Longarm finally managed to work his boot off, it was close to sunup. Bending himself back like a pretzel, he managed to unstrap the small leather holster containing the derringer and work it and the derringer into a corner behind the remains of a wooden bucket. There was no sense in trying to use it in his present condition. It would have to be his ace in the hole—or corner.

Totally exhausted by that time, he slept.

He awoke to find the door open and Telford and Mike standing over him, sunlight streaming in through the begrimed window to his right.

Mike paused just before him, his feet wide, his arms akimbo, grinning happily. "So this is the mighty Longarm," he said.

He strode forward suddenly and kicked Longarm, the narrow point of his boot digging cruelly into Longarm's side. Longarm gasped but did not cry out.

"He's a tough one, ain't he," commented Mike to Telford.

"He is that. Work him over. If you need any help, get Hank. I want to know what he's doin' up here. I don't like the idea of U. S. marshals nosing around this valley."

Mike wiped his mouth off with the back of his hand, his eyes lighting at the prospect. "Sure thing, Mr. Telford. But I don't think I'll need Hank. I can handle this son of a bitch all by myself."

"Then do it. We move out tonight. And before we

do, I want to know all that man can tell us."

Telford turned then and left Longarm to Mike. Mike closed the door and walked closer to Longarm. "That knifing made it certain I'd have to pay for a woman for the rest of my days, Longarm. It sure is nice I'm goin' to have a chance to pay you off for that."

"It was your knife. You came after me."

"Shut up."

Mike began to kick Longarm. All Longarm could do was curl up in a ball and try to last the man out. It was not easy, and soon the pain was so great Longarm thought he was going to lose consciousness. Before he did, Mike pulled back, panting. He was tiring of his game.

Longarm looked up at him. "Listen, Mike. Like I told Telford, I'm runnin' from the law, same as the rest of you."

Mike, still breathing heavily, pulled back. "You expect me to believe that?"

"How does four thousand in newly minted gold sound to you? That's what I got stashed away. I got sick of living on what the government was paying me. I'll split it with you."

A flash of pure greed leaped into Mike's eyes, to be replaced almost at once by a mean wariness. "Telford told me you said something about gold. He said you put what you took in a bank under your own name and got caught."

"I didn't put all of it in that bank."

"You're lyin'! You think I'd believe you? A federal marshal?"

"You never heard of one goin' bad before?"

"I never knew a man didn't have a price—and that's a fact. But I sure as hell figured you was different."

"When it comes to money, we're all alike. You should know that."

His shoulders still rising and falling steadily from his recent exertion, Mike wiped his mouth and studied Longarm carefully. "All right," he said. "Where'd you hide that money?"

"It's not in my saddlebag."

Mike stepped forward and kicked Longarm in the gut. The pain was so intense, Longarm blacked out momentarily. When he came out of it and looked up again at Mike, the bearded outlaw was smiling down at him.

"Don't get smart. Just tell me where that gold is."

"Let me up and I'll take you to it."

"It's near here?"

"Why the hell did you think I fought so hard to keep them Dennims from raising that stage? They didn't know why that leather valise in the rear boot was so heavy, but I did."

Longarm was inventing out of whole cloth now, but he knew that Mike Deaver had not been on that stage when the Dennims were robbing it, and knew little about it.

Mike was hooked now. "So where is it?"

"While the jehu and that gambler were lugging Hank Dennim's body to the side of the road, I was hiding that valise of gold in a place I'd found near the stream, under a boulder."

Mike frowned. "You mean you figured it would not be a good idea to bring the gold into Snake Flat?"

"Not after that attempted raise. There'd be too many eyes on me."

"Yeah. That makes sense."

"You'll need me to take you to it."

"Guess I will, at that."

Mike hunkered down beside Longarm and lit a cigar. Then he blew the smoke into Longarm's face and chuckled. "I'm goin' to have to make this look good, Longarm. Know what I mean?"

"No."

Mike punched Longarm on the side of the face. The blow almost dislocated Longarm's jaw and brought tears of fury into the corners of his eyes. But he said nothing.

"That's what I mean. I'll have to mess you up pretty good so Jake won't get suspicious. I'll tell him you stuck to your story, but I won't tell him about the gold. Then we'll move out tonight, the two of us. And you'll take me to that gold."

"And then you'll take it and kill me."

"I won't kill you. I don't think. But I will now right here in this bunkhouse if you don't agree to take me to that gold. See, this way, you get a chance to live a little longer for sure. Otherwise..." He shrugged and blew some more smoke into Longarm's face.

"I'll take you."

"Sure you will." Mike stood up and grinned down at Longarm and shook his head. "The mighty Longarm. You don't look like much right now, and that's a fact."

133

He began to kick Longarm. He worked hard at it, patiently seeking new angles, unprotected flanks. When this exhausted him, he began to punch Longarm about the head and shoulders. One punch mashed Longarm's lip. Another caused a freshet of blood to burst from one nostril. When Mike had beaten Longarm to the point where the lawman no longer felt much of anything, he pulled back wearily and called Carl into the room.

As the two men looked down at him, Longarm heard Mike tell Carl to get Telford. Longarm had not changed his story, Mike said.

That was all Longarm remembered.

Longarm awoke twice during that day. The first time was when Telford squatted down beside him while someone dumped a bucket of water over him, then left him alone with Telford. As Longarm shuddered and tried to peer through the streaming water at Telford, the big man smiled sadly.

"I'd like to believe you, Longarm," he said. "I surely would. The thing is, you'd stick out like a sore thumb now. Besides, you got any idea how many of my men—and how many other men in this valley— would like to get their hands on you? You'd be almost as good as a Pinkerton to them."

He chuckled at the thought and shook his head.

Longarm blinked away the water still resting in his eye sockets and peered at Telford past his swollen, battered cheeks and throbbing brows. "What are you runnin' from, Telford?" he managed.

"Why should I tell you, you poor son of a bitch?

134

It won't do you no good to find that out. That ain't your business any more. Right? Besides, you're already a dead man."

"You're gonna sic another one of your dogs on me, Telford?"

"Not my dogs, Longarm. I sent a rider after Pa Dennim to tell him we have you. He'll be riding in first thing tomorrow. I'll let him skin you alive and hang the bones out to dry. It won't bring Pa's boys back, but it will sure as hell make the old bear feel better."

Telford got to his feet, regarded the crumpled Longarm for a moment, then strode from the room. Longarm heard the key in the padlock, then the sound of the bar slamming down across the door. As Telford's footsteps faded, Longarm pushed himself into the corner and began groping for the small leather holster that contained his derringer.

The gun was still there. The fellow who had filled the wooden bucket hadn't seen it.

It was late when he was awakened for the second time. He heard the key in the padlock and sat up as well as he could with his hands still lashed together behind him. He could hear the racket the crickets were making in the grass outside. Stripes of moonlight lay across the muddy floor in front of him and partway up the door.

It swung open and Mike stepped inside.

"You say a word," Mike whispered, "and I'll slit your throat."

Longarm said nothing. Mike moved around behind

him and sliced through the rawhide binding his wrists, then cut the rawhide around his ankles.

"Put that boot back on," Mike told him. "And hurry it up. Our horses are waiting out back. You let out a sound and you're a dead man. I'll say I caught you tryin' to escape."

Longarm was pulling the boot on. He was having a difficult time. The circulation had not yet returned to his hands and he knew that he would have trouble standing, also. And something else. He had fouled himself in his sleep and the stench made him wince.

"Hurry it up!" Mike hissed.

"I can hardly use my hands and I won't be able to stand up until I get the circulation back."

"Rub the ankles then."

"And something else. I'll need clean pants."

"What the hell do you want me to do? Bring you a new wardrobe?"

"Bring me something."

"You got anything in your bedroll?"

"Yes."

"I'll get it." Before he slipped out the door, he paused. "Don't try anything, Longarm. You ain't in a good spot to raise a ruckus."

"I know that, damn it," responded Longarm, massaging his ankles and feet. "Just get me that bedroll."

Mike pulled the door shut and dropped the bar in place. As soon as Longarm heard him moving off, he kicked off his remaining boot and peeled off his long-johns and fouled buckskins, wiped himself as clean as he could, and flung the fouled clothing into a corner. Was there anything worse than the stench a hu-

136

man could make? Longarm wondered miserably. Then he reached over into the corner and grabbed up the holster containing the derringer and strapped it to the back of his leg.

Longarm was on his feet, his back resting against the outside wall, when Mike returned.

"Here," Mike said, flinging the bedroll at Longarm.

"Better keep a lookout," Longarm told him. "I think I heard someone prowling around in the next room before you came back."

Frowning, Mike kept guard at the door while Longarm pulled on fresh britches, then stepped into his boots. His hat was lying in a corner. He put it on.

"I'm ready," he said.

"Follow me," Mike said.

Longarm did not argue as he kept close behind Mike. Longarm's black was waiting alongside Mike's mount behind the bunkhouse, as Mike had promised. Longarm tied the bedroll on and swung into the saddle.

"Where's my Winchester and Colt?" he asked.

Astride his own mount beside Longarm, Mike drew his sixgun and cocked it. Pointing it at Longarm, he said, "Just move out. Head west into them hills. Then take me to that gold and don't ask no more questions. I got some thinkin' to do. About what I'm going to do with you—and all that gold."

Longarm clapped spurs to his black and moved out, heading for the dark hills surrounding the ranch.

• • •

They were out of the hills, moving along the stage road at least five miles south of Snake Flat, when Longarm pulled up. Mike, just behind him, put his horse alongside Longarm.

"Now what?" he demanded, his Colt out, the muzzle looking up into Longarm's face.

"My right foot is killing me. I can hardly keep it in the stirrup."

"What's wrong with it?"

"I never did get a chance to rub the circulation back into it. It's still asleep. Hurts like hell. I can hardly stay in the saddle."

"Forget it. Just keep ridin'. You're doin' fine."

With a weary shrug, Longarm nudged the black on. Mike holstered his weapon and fell in behind him. A mile or so farther on, Longarm pulled up again. This time, as Mike pulled his mount to a halt beside Longarm, he was not so pleasant.

"What the hell is it now?" he demanded.

"Same thing. I tell you, I got to get down and rub some blood into this foot."

"God damn it!"

"It won't take long."

"It better not!"

Longarm slipped carefully off the black. Then, limping grotesquely, he led the black into a light patch of timber alongside the road. He ground-reined the black, hobbled over to a boulder, and eased himself onto it. Mike stayed on his mount and watched for a few moments, then dismounted himself and walked over, leading his horse.

"You better not be tryin' to pull something," Mike warned, his Colt out. To emphasize his resolve, Mike cocked the hammer.

Longarm paid no heed to him as he tugged on his right foot. Mike watched him for a moment, then glanced down the moonlit coach road. "How much farther we got to go?" he demanded.

"Hell, I don't know this road all that well. I just rode over it that once. But there should be a grade farther on. On its crest was where the Dennims stopped us."

"You're right," Mike said, brightening. "I know the spot."

Longarm carefully placed his right boot down beside the boulder and began to massage his right ankle and foot gently. In the darkness, there was not much to see except Longarm's pale hands working feverishly to restore the circulation. Unable to curb his eagerness to reach the gold, Mike glanced once again down the road. The moment he did so, Longarm pushed himself away from the boulder and in one single motion brought up the derringer, tucking its twin bores under Mike's chin. Then he cocked the weapon.

"Oh, shit," Mike said.

"Drop the Colt."

Mike let it fall to the ground.

Perfectly healthy by this time, Longarm stepped back, then kicked Mike in the groin. When Mike ducked over, gasping, Longarm brought his knee up, driving it into Mike's face, destroying his nose. As Mike grabbed at his shattered nose and staggered back,

Longarm followed after him and brought the edge of his palm down on the side of Mike's neck. The rabbit punch caused Mike to sag weakly to the ground. Once he was on the ground, Longarm kicked him.

Astonished at his anger, Longarm pocketed the derringer, grabbed a fistful of Mike's hair, and lifted him off the ground. The man came up, gasping in pain. Longarm drove his right fist across the man's jaw. The jawbone cracked loudly and Mike went down as heavily as a sack of potatoes.

Longarm took one leg and dragged Mike deep into the timber. Mike's head kept slamming into stumps and boulders, but Longarm paid little attention. When he came upon a small hollow filled with pine needles, he pulled up and rolled Mike into the hollow. Examining Mike closely, he found the man was still very much alive. Vaguely disappointed, he went back to his horse for rope. When he returned, he ripped off Mike's shirt, stuffed a good deal of it into the man's mouth, then wrapped strips of it around Mike's already painfully swollen jaw so Mike couldn't spit out the gag. Longarm could see that Mike's jaw was certainly broken, but he didn't want to take any chances.

Once Mike was effectively gagged, Longarm rolled him over onto his stomach, tied both wrists behind him, then bound both ankles, after which he linked the wrists to the ankles with a single strand of rope, looped the rope twice around Mike's ankles, then brought the rope up and around Mike's neck, pulling it tight and knotting it securely.

Then he slapped Mike awake. The man tried to

straighten his legs out. At once he felt the rope's strands biting into his Adam's apple.

He gasped and drew his legs back. As he did this, he glared up at Longarm with murderous eyes.

Longarm smiled. He wished he had a cigar so he could blow smoke in Mike's face. "I'll be back for you, Mike," Longarm promised. "Soon's I finish up here. I don't know for sure how long that'll take, so just keep quiet and get plenty of sleep."

Still smiling, Longarm grabbed a fistful of Mike's hair and dragged him into the ditch. When Mike's body had sunk pretty far into the pine needles, Longarm kicked soil and pine needles over him until only Mike's head remained visible.

Feeling considerably better, Longarm returned to the black and started back north. It would take him until late in the morning, he figured, to reach the Saxons' ranch.

Unless, of course, he ran into more of Telford's men.

He reached the Saxon spread sooner than he had expected, and rode into the compound leading Mike's horse. Mike's Colt was sitting in his holster, and the man's Winchester rested in his boot.

By the time he reached the main house, a fine, two-story frame dwelling with a broad veranda that swept around two sides of the house, a number of ranch hands were standing in the compound watching. As he pulled up wearily in front of the house, Dan

Saxon appeared on the porch, Rose Gantry beside him.

"Where the hell did you come from?" Saxon boomed heartily.

"My God, Custis," said Rose, her face filled with concern, "you look terrible. What happened to you?"

Rita appeared on the veranda beside her father. Her face instantly reflected the same concern Rose had shown. "Are you all right, Mr. Long?" she cried.

Longarm slipped wearily off the black. "I'm fine," he replied. "What I'd like first off is a bath and a chance to get out of these clothes." He grinned crookedly at Rita. "That offer of forty dollars and found still good?"

"Of course it is," she said.

Mounting the veranda steps, Longarm pulled up in front of Saxon. "How many men can you get together, Saxon?"

"Why . . ." the man frowned, surprised by the suddenness of the query. "That depends. Why do you ask?"

"You're going to have visitors. Telford's making his move on you tonight. He doesn't plan to leave much of anything standing when he rides out of here."

"I've been expecting this. Are you certain, Long?"

"I'm certain."

"Then I'll send for the other ranchers. We'll make a stand!"

"Send for them now. You don't have much time." Longarm looked at Rita. "What about that bath?" he asked her, his voice sounding oddly hollow to his ears.

She reached out for him. He took a step toward her, weariness smiting him suddenly. His limbs felt as heavy as tree trunks. Patches of darkness swam before his eyes, and the next thing he knew, he was being helped into the house and up what seemed like a very long flight of stairs.

Chapter 9

Longarm awoke quickly, alertly. Someone was bending over him. Opening his eyes, he saw it was Rita.
She was wearing a blue cotton shirt open at the neck
and Levi's. Her dark hair coiled down about her shoulders. This, he realized, was her ranch costume.

"How do you feel?" she asked.

"How long have I been out?"

"Two hours. You must have been exhausted. And
your face has been all beaten."

"Not only that, but it was done on purpose."

Longarm sat up. He had been stripped naked. The
clean, freshly ironed sheets felt cool and soothing
against his battered hide.

"Who undressed me?" he asked Rita.

"I did."

"I need a bath."

"I know. The tub's been brought in. Are you ready for it?"

He looked over and saw the high-backed porcelain tub. There were roses and other flowers imprinted on its side. A woman's tub.

"Will that be big enough for me?"

"If you scrunch down."

"Bring on the hot water."

She smiled and vanished from the room. Longarm got up and walked over to the window. He was in time to see two parties of horsemen riding into the compound. As they dismounted in front of the barn, Dan Saxon greeted them. Saxon was getting his forces together.

Longarm walked back to the bed and sat down on it, his brow creased in a frown. He was wondering if his escape with Mike Deaver might cause Telford to cancel the attack on Circle S he had planned for this night. It should not have that effect unless Telford knew that Longarm was going to warn Saxon. And there was no way Telford could know that. How could Telford have guessed that Longarm had overheard his roistering ranch hands discussing the upcoming attack?

The door opened and a fat Indian housekeeper tramped in as silent as the passage of time and poured a steaming kettle of water into the bathtub. A moment later a girl who appeared to be her daughter brought up another kettle. Neither one of them glanced in his direction, though he sat on the edge of the bed stark naked.

The procession continued until the tub was filled. Rita entered with a bar of soap, a brush, and an armload of towels.

"All ready," she said, nodding toward the steaming water.

"I can bathe myself," he told her.

"I know you can. But you can't scrub your own back."

Longarm realized the truth of that. He also realized that by this time it would be silly for him to attempt to hide his nakedness from her. He got to his feet, walked calmly past her, and peered down at the hot, steaming water. Gingerly, he lifted his foot and allowed one big toe to test its temperature.

The toe protested.

"It's too hot," Longarm said.

"Wait awhile."

He stepped back. The door opened and the Indian housekeeper and her daughter trooped in with two more kettles of boiling water.

"Put them down over there," Rita said, indicating a spot directly behind the tub.

They did so silently, then turned and marched out.

"Try it now," Rita said.

Longarm did. This time he was satisfied. He stepped into the tub and eased his long frame down into the near-scalding water. It felt magnificent. The small tub crowded him, however, and by the time his bony flanks reached the bottom of the tub, his knees were up as high as his chin. But the water felt too good to protest.

Suddenly Rita was soaping his head. Stinging suds

flowed down over his forehead and into the corners of his eyes. He closed them tightly and splashed hot water into them to relieve the sting as Rita's surprisingly strong fingers began to massage his scalp. Abruptly she shoved his head forward through his knees. Gasping, he felt the water close over his head. He lifted his head, blowing like a beached whale. Rita pushed it down again.

This time he was ready and let her. She pulled his head out, soaped him some more, then pushed him down again to rinse off the soap. Releasing his head at last, she stepped back. Longarm was about to say something when a cascade of steaming water pounded down over his head. As the steam billowed up around him, he was almost certain she had scalded him to death.

She paid no heed to his panic as she began scrubbing his back with the brush. It felt delightful. As she scrubbed over his shoulders and down his chest and across his flat washboard of a stomach, she made no effort to hide her pleasure at contemplating Longarm's generous endowments. Her flushed face came close to Longarm's, and he found himself able to peer down her open shirt front. She was not wearing a corset, he noticed. This knowledge caused his throat to tighten somewhat, and he looked quickly away.

She smiled at him, her teeth flashing brilliantly in her olive face. With an impulsive movement, her hand reached down and felt him.

Her eyebrows shot up in amazement.

"Easy there," he said.

"Do you still think I am a virgin?" she asked,

resuming her scrubbing of his stomach.

"I'm not sure now," Longarm admitted.

"Is that why you left me alone in your room? Because you thought I was a virgin?"

"Yes."

"When I asked why that should matter, you left so quickly you gave me no chance to explain. I was very angry. And hurt."

"I'm sorry, Rita."

"I am not a virgin, Custis. When you asked the question I was surprised. I wondered why such a consideration should matter to you. Now I think I understand. You are what they call a gentleman."

"Believe me, it's not easy sometimes."

She smiled again, dazzlingly. "I can understand why." She got to her feet. "You can stand up now," she said.

Longarm pushed himself to his full height. Rita saw what the effect of her closeness had been, but said not a word as she busied herself scrubbing down his buttocks and the back of his legs. She was very thorough. Longarm could feel the miles of dust peeling off, and a good pound of skin going with it. Another steaming bucket of hot water rinsed him, then she folded a huge towel around him and helped him to step out of the tub.

She patted him all over. His body tingled. The Indian housekeeper entered and placed slippers and a robe on the bed. His longjohns, stockings, and buckskin shirt and pants had disappeared. With the towel wrapped discreetly around his long frame, Longarm was led by Rita over to the bed. "Wait a minute," she said, and went over to the door and locked it.

Then she returned to him and pushed him gently down on the bed. He came to rest on his back, looking up at Rita. Something else was looking up at her, too.

"Roll over," she told him, "unless you're afraid you'll break it off."

"Just have to chance it," he replied, rolling over.

Longarm felt the bed jounce slightly as she climbed up beside him and began working on the muscles about his neck and shoulders. Her hands pounded gently at first, then gained in power and assertiveness. The edges of her palms were like blunt knives as they kneaded his muscles and moved down his back.

It was incredibly soothing. He felt the tension in his body fade. His senses drifted off as the magic of Rita's fingers and hands continued to play over the length of his body. As her fingers dug into the calves of his legs, they were like steel, but soothing to a marvelous degree.

Longarm closed his eyes and rested his head to one side. He was almost asleep when she rolled him over gently onto his back and dropped her face to his. He opened his mouth just as her lips closed about his lower lip. She sucked on it, her tongue flicking it. Then she rolled over onto him and let her tongue dart deep into his mouth. He was startled to find that she was as naked from the waist down as he was. During her expert massage, she had somehow managed to kick off her boots and wriggle out of her Levi's. He stopped kissing her, reached up, and in a trice he peeled her shirt off.

"You must think me shameless," she whispered.

"Right now, all I can think of is what a big improvement this is over the last couple of days."

She laughed softly and took his face in her hands, leaned still closer to him, and kissed him again on the mouth, her lips probing his. She moaned from deep within her, then thrust her tongue into his mouth. He rolled over onto her and ground his naked body against hers. She began to writhe, moaning softly, her lips still fastened to his. He brought his hands up to cup her warm breasts. His rough fingertips caressed the nipples. Her moan grew in intensity as her arms tightened around his neck, her tongue still probing deliciously. He could smell her. It was not perfume, but the sweet, maddening aroma of a woman aroused. It filled his nostrils, arousing him to an even keener pitch.

He broke the kiss and took one of her nipples in his mouth. It swelled even larger and grew as hard as a bullet. His tongue flicked it expertly. Rita leaned back, moaning softly, then reached down and grabbed him. His huge readiness astonished her. He heard her gasp, and chuckled deeply, then thrust his own hand down between her thighs. She opened her legs eagerly. His probing fingers thrust themselves deep into her crotch, then past her moist, pliant lips.

"Now!" she pleaded huskily. "Enter me now! I'm ready!"

With his big hands he thrust her buttocks under him as he moved between her splayed legs. He went in full and deep.

"Yes!" Rita breathed. "Yes! But go deeper, Custis! Deeper!"

Longarm did his best to oblige. He pulled away for a tantalizing instant, leaving just the tip of his erection inside her, then plunged deliberately, powerfully, even more deeply than he had been able to go before.

Rita uttered a sharp, guttural cry that seemed wrung from the very depths of her soul. She swung up her legs and locked her ankles around his neck as he continued to thrust. Then she cried out in pleasure.

"Oh, that's it! Keep going! Faster!"

After a dozen deep thrusts, Longarm felt her juices begin to flow out around the base of his erection. Her cries of excitement grew even more intense. With each shattering plunge, her ecstasy mounted, her cries quicker, shorter, like yelps—and it all had its effect on Longarm. He was also pounding toward orgasm.

Abruptly Rita became rigid under him. Her ankles tightened around his neck. He bunched his neck muscles to protect himself and hung on. Her inner muscles squeezed convulsively and began milking his erection. In that instant he thrust powerfully and came, in a sudden, overwhelming outpouring.

Rita sighed, uttering a long exhalation of breath. She let her legs drop to the bed. Gasping, Longarm fell forward upon her glistening body and lay with his head resting on the pillow of her breasts. After a second or two, when he had regained his breath, he lifted his head to look at her.

He frowned. Rita's eyes were closed and she was barely breathing.

"Rita!" he whispered. "Rita! What's wrong?"

She did not respond. Her face was deathly white.

Frantically, he pressed his ear against her mouth and was not sure he could feel her breathing. He shook her. An eyelid fluttered. He took a deep, grateful breath and leaned back. Her face flushed suddenly and both eyes opened. She looked at him and smiled.

"My, that was nice," she breathed dreamily.

"You passed out!"

"Yes. I should have warned you. I do that sometimes. When it's good. Very, very good."

"It scared me."

"It needn't. Just means you did a fine job."

He started to get up.

"Where are you going?"

He laughed. "Haven't you had enough?"

"Do you know how rare my trips to Cheyenne are, Longarm? You're not getting away that easily. Come here!"

She drew him down and kissed him lingeringly while her hand dropped down and began manipulating him expertly. He felt himself stir to life once again, amazed. She felt him at once and laughed. Then she swung out from under him smoothly and mounted him from the top, falling forward heavily, gasping with pleasure as she felt him slip deeper and deeper into her. In a moment, he was as good as new, and she looked down at him with her eyes shining in delight.

She leaned back, gasping with pleasure, and soon their bodies were locked together and there was no room left for him to probe. Squeezing delightedly with the muscles in her buttocks, she began rotating her hips very, very slowly. Longarm relaxed and let it happen. Rita knew precisely what she was doing, prolonging it as much as was humanly possible, pausing in her hip rotations more and more often, for shorter and shorter periods, as she succumbed to her own mounting pleasure.

Abruptly, her long hair streaming down over Longarm's face and shoulders, she began rocking herself back and forth until at last, with a deep groan, she poured her juices down over him in a hot, delicious explosion that sent her falling forward upon his chest, limp and trembling.

But, fortunately, not unconscious.

"Lie back and relax, Rita," he told her.

She murmured a sleepy response. Longarm had held himself back with steely control, intent only on her pleasure. Now, still inside her, he rolled her over and plunged even deeper, impaling her on the bed, then began thrusting with full, slow, even strokes. He was determined not to hurry, and used only a part of his weight and strength. He had told her to lie back and relax, and that was just what she did for the first few minutes.

But gradually she came to life under him. Longarm felt her inner muscles responding to his measured, metronomic thrusts. She began to lunge up at him to meet his downward strokes. Soon she was moving faster, driving up at him still harder. Tiny cries of delight began to escape from her. She kept her eyes shut tightly and began to snap her head back and forth.

Longarm himself was on his own now, building to the final moment. It had been a long time coming, for both of them, but by this time their bodies were slamming at each other with a heedless, mindless urgency. He passed the point of no return, pulsing out of control, throbbing, emptying into her. He heard Rita's tough, short grunts as her body pulsed in unison with his, then thrashed wildly under him as she clung to him and sucked him into her. Abruptly, her body arched. She cried out in a kind of aching sob as Longarm, still pulsing inside her, continued to empty himself.

At last, completely drained, he dropped heavily upon her, his face again resting on the two snowy mounds of her breasts. He was utterly spent. When his breathing quieted, he lifted his head and looked at Rita. A rosy flush was once again spreading over her face, and her eyes flickered open.

"Wow," she murmured happily, running her fingers idly through his damp hair. "Twice in the same day! That was nice, Custis. Very nice."

Longarm shifted his weight off her. She turned and snuggled up close to him.

"Don't leave," she said.

"Do I have any choice?"

"What do you mean?"

"Didn't I see riders dismounting in the yard?"

She frowned. "Yes. Dad did what you told him. He sent for the other ranchers. The ones we can count on."

"Then I'd better get down there."

"I suppose so. But not right away."

"No," he said, kissing her gently on her cheek. "Not right away."

• • •

Longarm sat listening in a corner astride a chair, his forearms across its back, his chin resting on them. The big kitchen was crowded with cattlemen, and Dan Saxon had just told them what Longarm had found out during his short stay as a guest at the T Bar.

Longarm had not told Saxon under what circumstances he had been brought to Telford's place and how he had left.

There were four ranchers in all, plus Ogden Maxwell. When Longarm entered, the men had become exceedingly nervous, and not one of them had wanted to look Longarm squarely in the eyes. For the first time, it dawned on the lawman that more than one outlaw had found a home in this valley, and he wondered if his true identity had as yet found its way to these ranchers. He sure as hell hoped not.

Phil Olsen was the owner of the Jinglebob. He sat alongside Saxon at the table, the lower part of his face hidden by a rich black beard he kept trimmed just below his jawline. When he smiled, his teeth flashed like summer lightning in a thundercloud. He was speaking now.

". . . so that means Telford's got the manpower he needs. All we got is this here warning."

"That's enough to give us the advantage," Saxon insisted.

"That's right," said Clem Jenks, who was sitting across the table from Saxon. "It might be all we need."

Jenks was the owner of the Dewlap, the closest ranch to the Circle S. He was a wiry man with curly red hair and wild, beetling eyebrows. He seemed the most combative of the bunch, but Longarm had long since learned to discount appearances. The only time action counted was when it was needed.

"So we need a plan," drawled Bob Steele, the owner of the Double B. He leaned back and eyed Saxon. "You got one?"

"Long has." Saxon nodded to Longarm. "You want to tell them?" he asked.

Longarm got up from his chair and walked over to the table. He sat down facing Saxon and alongside Rod McCracken of the Lazy M. "Sure," he said. "It's simple enough. We send the women to town, leave this ranch wide open, draw Telford and his men in, then open up on them. Cut them down to a man. We might even end up chasing them back to their hole."

"That'd be nice," said Steele. He was a hefty, full-throated fellow with a broad chest and an easy, booming laugh. His voice and his manner were serious now as he stared across the table at Longarm. "But maybe it's just a little too easy."

McCracken stirred himself and turned to glance at Longarm. A lean, bald man with a prominent Adam's apple and startlingly blue eyes, he had said nothing since entering the kitchen. That he was about to speak now made everyone suddenly attentive.

"There might be damage to the Circle S," he said. "Considerable damage. And how are you going to be sure Telford will take the bait? If he sees no lights, the place deserted, won't he suspect something?"

"He sure as hell will," Longarm admitted. "That's why we'll keep some lights on. And why there will be a few of us moving around. There'll be activity—just enough to draw Telford and his men in."

McCracken looked across the table at Saxon. "What do you think, Dan? You willin' to chance it?"

Before Saxon could reply, Ogden Maxwell cleared his throat to speak for the first time. From the moment he had entered the kitchen, it had been apparent to Longarm that Maxwell was no longer—if he ever had been—the easygoing booster he had appeared when he first approached Longarm in the Bagdad saloon. "I say we do it, Dan," Maxwell said, his voice sharp and powerful. "I don't see how we'll ever get as good a chance again to stop Telford in his tracks."

"I agree, Max."

Steele spoke up. "I say we do it."

Saxon looked around the table. "Everyone in?"

The four ranchers nodded solemnly.

"Good. Now for the details." Saxon leaned forward and glanced quickly around the table. "I know what manpower you got, so here's how I think we should spread our forces..."

Chapter 10

The sky was cloudless. The moon was out and the stars gleamed in the heavens. Yet the night was filled with thunder.

Crouched in the bunkhouse, Longarm peered out through a grimy window. As he watched, a dim figure left the main house and hurried across the compound toward the barn. Phil Olsen and his six Jinglebob riders were in there waiting. The cabin door opened, sending a splash of yellow light over the front yard. Then it was pulled shut again.

Everyone was doing his part, showing just enough activity to bring Telford's riders into the trap. Longarm saw a few riders now, moving shapes on the crest of a hill north of the ranch. They were pouring down toward the compound, the thunder of their hooves growing louder with each passing second.

Longarm blew out the two lanterns and slipped from the bunkhouse. Darting across the compound, he circled behind the barn, then followed the creek until he came to the plank bridge crossing it. He passed the Dewlap riders crouching in the grass and found Clem Jenks where he had left him earlier, positioned behind a bush in the cottonwoods on the other side of the bridge. The man was busy loading an enormous Walker Colt. As Longarm ducked down beside him, he glanced at him, a grin on his face.

"They're comin'," he chuckled. "Hear that thunder? They took the bait, sure enough. Who was that in the house opened the door like that?"

"Max."

"Real clever," Clem said.

"How many do you figure?" Longarm was peering into the flat. He could barely see them coming, but he could hear them easy enough.

"They split up after they crested the hills. Looks like maybe ten riders coming through here. The rest'll be crossing the creek farther down to come in behind the barn."

"All right. Remember, wait until this bunch is across the bridge before opening up."

Clem patted the big Colt's nine-inch barrel and nodded.

Keeping low, Longarm moved swiftly on through the cottonwoods, checking to make sure the other men he and Saxon had positioned earlier were ready. They were. Eight of McCracken's men were waiting with

McCracken, and they were nicely spread out. They had been waiting patiently for the attack since midnight, and seemed eager now to get this over with. For a while Longarm had begun to wonder if Telford had decided to call it off.

Apparently, he had not.

Steele was positioned with his men at the entrance to the small valley, Olsen and McCracken with a sizable crew in the flat just north of the creek. Any that got through either force and tried to make it back across the creek and into the hills would run into Steele's men. By now Telford must have passed Steele's men. The trap had already been sprung.

Longarm picked a spot near the edge of the cottonwoods and levered a round into his Winchester. He could see the riders now, sweeping in a long curve toward the bridge. Someone was running toward him from the direction of the ranch house. He glanced back and saw Maxwell, a rifle in his hands. Longarm waved. Maxwell veered toward him. Nodding grimly, he settled down beside him, peering through the night at the oncoming riders.

"I thought I heard them coming," he grunted.

"You heard them, all right. They split up like we figured they would. Jenks won't fire until they're all across the bridge."

"Good," Max said. "We won't have no trouble hearin' that cannon of his."

"I only hope it don't blow itself apart—and Jenks with it."

Max did not reply. Longarm settled deeper into the grass. The riders were pounding over the bridge now,

161

and Longarm saw the unlit torches some of them were carrying. They had come to burn and kill. As the last of them crossed the bridge, the night was shattered by the detonation of Clem Jenks's Walker Colt.

It was the signal the men had been waiting for. The night exploded. A withering fusillade of shots poured into Telford's riders as they charged through the cottonwoods toward the compound. The shouts of angry, wounded men filled the night. Longarm saw two riders, frantic to escape the trap, whipping their horses in his direction.

Beside him, Max chuckled. Longarm lifted his rifle, sighted, and fired. The nearest rider tumbled back off his horse. Max fired and the other rider vanished. Four riders behind those two veered swiftly away, heading back toward the bridge. A flurry of shots brought them down as well.

Jumping up, Longarm said, "Let's get over to help Olsen!"

Nodding, Max struggled to his feet and raced along beside Longarm. He was puffing mightily by the time they reached the compound. The riders who had come in behind the barn had been cut to pieces by Phil Olsen's bunch waiting for them in the barn. Some were still on their horses, milling about, shooting at shadows, others had been hit and were writhing on the ground, crying out.

Out of the swirling mass a rider emerged, heading for Longarm. "Mine," Longarm said, lifting his Winchester. He sighted and fired. The rider flung out both hands and was swept off his horse. The riderless mount charged past Longarm and disappeared into the night.

Gunfire was coming from every direction now as the battle broke down into individual firefights. Longarm and Max ducked low and then edged back toward the cottonwoods, waiting for targets of opportunity. Levering another shell into firing position, Longarm turned his head to peer into the gloom of the cottonwoods. The sound of gunfire from the trees had become sporadic. Then a wedge of three horsemen burst out of the cottonwoods, heading straight for Longarm and Max. At the same time, a cloud passed across the moon, plunging the compound into darkness.

"Down!" cried Longarm as the three riders thundered out of the blackness toward them.

Lying flat, Longarm brought up his rifle and fired at the foremost rider. He could not be sure, it was so dark—but the rider looked like Jake Telford. Longarm's shot seemed to have no effect, however, as the lead rider spurred his horse immediately to Longarm's right, pulling the other riders after him.

As they passed Longarm, they poured a fusillade down at the two men. One slug whispered past Longarm's neck, and he heard Max gasp in sudden pain. As the three riders swept on past, Longarm got to his feet and flung another shot at them. One rider pitched sideways off his horse. From the ground at Longarm's feet, Max fired twice, managing to bring down another rider. But the lead rider kept going, roweling his horse furiously.

Someone near the barn shouted a warning. Longarm turned in time to see another horseman galloping toward him out of the cottonwoods. The moon was sailing in a clear sky once again, and Longarm saw who this rider was: Pa Dennim. His huge bulk loomed high over the neck of his mount like a grizzly bear.

Firing from his hip, Dennim blasted the Winchester from Longarm's hand. His right hand stinging fiercely, Longarm reached out as Dennim swept past and grabbed the old man's thigh with both hands. Dennim came flying from the saddle. He hit the ground heavily. Longarm drew his Colt and clubbed Dennim on the side of the head. But it was not enough. Dennim twisted away from Longarm, staggered to his feet, and brought up his Colt.

Longarm fired first. The man staggered back, his gun hand wavering.

"Damn your eyes!" Dennim growled thickly.

He tried to raise his Colt. Longarm stepped forward and snatched it from him. Dennim pawed out blindly at Longarm, took one hesitant step forward, then plunged face down into the grass.

Longarm swore bitterly. He had not wanted to kill Pa Dennim. But the old man, like his sons, had simply not given him any alternative.

Another rider clattered from the cottonwoods. This rider was heading for the ranch house, a flaming torch brandished high. It was Carl—Mike Deaver's hatchet-faced friend—and he seemed doggedly, insanely determined to carry this attack through.

Longarm tried to bring him down with his Colt, but he galloped on past him toward the house. From a window a shot lanced out. Carl pulled up abruptly and started to whirl the torch over his head. Another shot exploded from the same window. Carl bucked and let the torch fall. Then he slid from his horse.

But he had not yet given up. He snatched up the guttering torch and began to run brokenly toward the ranch house. He was almost to the porch when one final shot cut him down.

This time, he lay where he had fallen.

Longarm looked back to the cottonwoods. The sound of firing from within them had ceased. A moment later Saxon's men came streaming out, their smoking guns in their hands.

"We got them!" one of the men cried as he pulled up beside Longarm. "Jesus! We really caught them with their pants down!"

"The place stinks of blood in there," another said wearily. Sweat was running down his face, and there was an angry crease already scabbing across his forehead. His face shone deathly white in the darkness.

"I don't know," another of the men said. "It was too dark in there to tell. It was pretty damn confusing, I can tell you."

"What about Telford?" Longarm asked.

Saxon appeared from the cottonwoods. He looked very weary. It was he who answered Longarm as he hurried across the compound toward him. "I think he got away," he said. "Him and two other riders broke right past us."

Longarm nodded grimly and turned to look in the direction the remaining horsemen had taken. If he crossed the creek further down and stayed on the course, he would miss Steele's waiting men—and a single horseman could easily make it into the hills without being challenged.

Damn it! Longarm had wanted Telford. With nothing now to gain by lying, he might have been willing to admit who he was and go back with Longarm. He had nothing left here to stay for. He had precipitated a range war and been soundly defeated. His tenure in this valley was at an end.

The distant rattle of gunfire came to the growing crowd of Saxon's men congregating around Longarm and Saxon. Grins creased grimy faces. They all knew what that firing meant. Steele and the others were closing the trap, rounding up the fleeing remnants of Telford's force. If they had captured Telford, the victory would have been complete.

"Saxon!"

It was Max. He did not sound good.

Longarm turned. Max was still on the ground. He was sitting up, but just barely. Saxon hurried over to him, Longarm following with the others.

"Where are you hit?" Saxon asked anxiously, dropping beside his old friend.

"In the gut. And it's there to stay." He managed a weak smile. "Did we take them bastards or did we take them?"

Saxon nodded eagerly. "We took them. Telford's gone, but he's finished in these parts, Max. We outlasted the bastard."

"You mean *you* did."

"Hell, Max. Don't talk like that." Saxon looked up at the faces crowding around. "Help me get him inside!"

As four men bent and carried the gutshot Maxwell gently into the house, Saxon sent a rider into town for a doctor. As Longarm watched the Circle S hand dash for the barn to get a horse, he realized grimly that it wasn't only Ogden Maxwell who needed a doctor. The dark compound's ground resembled a Civil War battlefield. From the cottonwoods came the dim, feeble cries of wounded and dying men.

Longarm turned and hurried toward the barn for his black. He intended to end this business as soon as possible. And that meant bearding Telford in his den before the man had a chance to recover.

Riding hard, Longarm reached the T Bar not long after Telford. As Longarm clattered into the compound, he caught Telford on his way into the ranch house. Halfway across the porch, the man swung around at Longarm's approach. He looked to be in bad shape. A bullet had nicked his left arm, and his face was drawn with the misery of defeat.

When Telford saw who it was, he clawed for his sixgun. "Damn you!" he cried. "I saw you there! You were the one who warned Saxon."

He hauled up his sixgun and fired—but the hammer came down on an empty chamber. Furious, he flung the gun from him and plunged into the house. Dismounting, Longarm drew his Colt and followed after him.

Once through the main door, he paused to orient himself. There was a single lamp lit in the living room. Marie was scrunched into the corner of the sofa, petrified.

"Where is he?" Longarm asked her.

"Upstairs," she whispered.

Longarm took the steps two at a time. The door at

the head of the stairs was ajar. With the barrel of his Colt, he nudged it open all the way, then stepped into the doorway.

Telford was standing by a desk with a shotgun in his hand.

Longarm ducked back out of the doorway as both barrels thundered. The plaster on the stairwell wall splintered as the buckshot slammed into it. Crouching unscathed outside the door, Longarm heard Telford break open the shotgun. He flung himself into the room, his Colt blasting. The first round caught Telford in his right shoulder, the second one in the thigh. As the man rocked back, he dropped the shotgun and the two shells he had been trying to drop into the barrels.

Longarm cocked his Colt a third time and steadied his aim on Telford's forehead. The man reached out to the desk for support, then sagged back into a swivel chair he had pushed out earlier from behind his desk. A weak smile creased his face.

"Go ahead, you son of a bitch," he said. "Finish it. I been runnin' long enough. I'm through in this valley anyway."

Longarm straightened up and holstered the .44.

"I guess I won't do that, Babe," Longarm told him, walking up to him and smiling down at the bleeding cattleman. A quick look at the man's wounds told him neither would likely prove fatal, though that probably didn't make them any the less painful.

"Babe?" Telford said, peering up at Longarm. "Is that what you called me?"

"That's right. Babe Warner. Train robber extraordinary, from what I hear."

"Well, mister," said Telford, "you don't hear well." Telford tried to smile, but began coughing raggedly instead.

"You denying who you are?"

"Okay. My name ain't Jake Telford. I'll admit that. The name my Pa let me use has got too many Pinkertons looking for it, and that's a fact. But, mister, it's also a fact that I am not Babe Warner. I never robbed a train in my life. A damn fool occupation that. Embezzlement was my game—at which there was none better."

Longarm frowned. For some reason, he found it easy to believe Telford's denial. "Do you happen to know a man called Pete Bowdoin?"

Telford's eyes lit with sudden dismay. "He the one fingered me?"

"He's the one."

Telford shook his head. "My own fault," he said. "I got too greedy."

"Maybe you better explain that."

"I'm hurtin', Marshal. Give me a hand, will you?"

"Where to?"

"My bed's in the next room. And I'm bleedin' like a stuck pig."

Longarm reached down and helped the man walk from his office to his bedroom across the hall. Then he called down to Marie. She came running, took one look at Telford, and hustled back downstairs to the kitchen to get what she needed.

A moment later, while Marie cut off Telford's shirt and trouser leg and began washing out his wounds with soap and water, Telford proceeded to tell Longarm why Pete Bowdoin had set Telford up. It was over a woman. Naturally.

". . . so how was I to know Pete was sweet on her? She was new to the Bagdad, and she and I hit it off from the beginning. When I heard Pete had sort of staked her out for himself, I just shrugged. He came at me a couple of times, but I slapped him around, and I thought that ended it."

"But it didn't."

"No. Not when the girl tried to get rid of a baby. She botched the job and died upstairs in the Bagdad. I did what I could for her, but it wasn't enough. The best doc in the territory couldn't have stopped all that bleeding."

"Pete blamed you?"

"That's right. He started making threats. It became a real nuisance, Marshal."

"So you went after him."

"I sent a couple of my boys after him."

"Like Mike Deaver and Carl."

Telford nodded grimly. "Them's the two I sent, God help me. Last I heard, he'd left the valley."

"And you thought you was through with him."

Telford smiled thinly. Marie had finished with the other wounds and was now wrapping the one on his arm. The man was obviously in considerable pain, the initial shock of the bullet wounds having worn off by this time. "That's right," he said, "but I wasn't, after all, was I? He sent you."

"Then you're not Babe Warner."

"Sorry, Marshal. I cannot claim the honor."

170

Longarm took a shot in the dark. "Then who in this valley *is* Babe Warner?"

Telford smiled. "Hell, Marshal, you just got through pullin' his chestnuts out of the fire."

"Saxon?"

"That's right. Dan Saxon. Ogden Maxwell was the brains of his outfit, but it was Saxon who pulled off all them train robberies. Saxon and I got to this valley about the same time and been feudin' ever since. Pete Bowdoin was a member of Dan's gang, but he couldn't have been much of one, I'm thinking."

Longarm nodded. It made sense, all right. Hell, nothing was ever as it seemed. He had learned that much, at least.

The sound of riders straggling into the compound came up to him. He went to the window and looked down. Three riders, their shoulders hunched in defeat, were riding across the compound, heading for the bunkhouse.

Longarm turned back to Telford. "Your defeated troops are returning."

"I can hear them."

Marie finished wrapping the bandage around Telford's arm and stepped back. Grateful for a chance to move, Telford stirred and tried to sit up. The exertion brought a spasm of pain that caused him to groan slightly and close his eyes for a minute.

Marie watched. There were tears in her eyes.

Telford opened his eyes and looked at her. "Marie, you think you can get one of the men to hitch up that buggy downstairs?"

171

She nodded.

"Then I guess you're going to have to drive me into Snake Flat to see the doc. Someone's got to take out this bullet in my shoulder."

As soon as Marie vanished out the door, Longarm said, "I'll help you down the stairs."

"Much obliged, Marshal."

Telford was barely conscious by the time Longarm lifted him into the buggy seat beside Marie. A few more T Bar riders drifted in while Longarm folded a blanket around Telford. Telford roused himself long enough to tell them what he had told the others—to clear out. He was finished in this valley. His riders took the news laconically and went on to the bunkhouse to pick up their gear.

As Marie slapped the horses with the reins and started up, two T Bar riders mounted up and fell in beside the buggy to provide an escort. Oddly pleased to see that, Longarm watched as Telford disappeared into the darkness on its way to Snake Flat.

Terry Dennim had come for the body of her father. When Longarm rode up late that next morning, he saw her sitting on the porch while two of Saxon's men hefted the dead man into the back of her buggy.

Beside her on the porch sat Rita, trying to comfort the girl. Dismounting in front of the ranch house, Longarm mounted the veranda steps and stopped in front of Terry.

"Your Pa died hard, Terry," Longarm told her. "There was nothing I could do to stop him from coming after me."

"I know it," she said, her face drawn, the light gone from her eyes. "Maybe someday I'll get even with you, Marshal. You never told me you was a lawman."

"Where'd you hear it?"

"From Pa. Now everyone knows it."

Longarm looked at Rita. She could not meet his eyes. The fact that he was a lawman changed everything, it seemed.

One of the two men who had loaded Pa Dennim into the wagon called up to Terry. She got up from her chair and moved past Longarm down the steps. Before she climbed up onto the seat, she turned and looked up at Longarm.

"Pa should've let me kill you."

Longarm said nothing. Terry turned, snatched up the reins, and sent the wagon on its way. He watched her as she drove out of the compound. He could understand her hatred. In a way, he could even admire it. For now, it was all she had to sustain her.

He turned to Rita. "Your father inside?"

"Yes. Ogden Maxwell died soon after you left last night. Dad took it pretty hard."

"I can imagine."

"But you can go in if you want. I'm sure Dad will want to see you."

Longarm nodded and went into the house. Saxon was in the living room, sitting with Rose Gantry beside the body of Ogden Maxwell. Max's large body took up the entire sofa. Saxon got up when Longarm entered and walked toward him. Rose got up also. She greeted Longarm with cold reserve and left the room.

There was a wary look in Saxon's eyes. "I been hearing things about you, Long."

"And I been hearing things about you, Babe."

The man's face paled slightly, but he took it in stride. "Who told you?"

"Telford."

"You believe him?"

"Yes."

"I see. So now I come with you, do I?" Saxon asked.

"What can you tell me about Mike Deaver and his buddy Carl? They both worked for Telford."

"They were bad ones."

"How bad?"

"Carl was wanted for murder. So is Deaver. Carl killed a landlady in Tucson with a butcher knife. I think she woke him up too early one morning."

"And Deaver?"

"A year ago in Utah he killed a couple of prospectors for their gold, then raped a settler's wife on his way here."

"Before he grew his beard."

Saxon nodded.

"About these other ranchers? They all got troubles, too?"

"What I tell you now I will deny in court."

"You won't have to. Do they?" Longarm asked.

"Yes."

"And, like you, they're trying to put down roots in this valley—a valley the railroad will soon make respectable."

"That's about it."

Longarm clapped his hat back on. "Maybe it would be nice if you could make Telford's exit from this valley as graceful as possible."

"You ain't takin' me in?"

"You going to admit to a judge who you are?"

"Never."

"And I guess it's pretty late to dig up witnesses of train robberies that took place so long ago."

Saxon began to brighten. "I guess that's true, at that."

"Besides, Pete Bowdoin says Babe Warner was Telford anyway."

"Pete?"

"That's right."

"He the one sent you up here?"

"He's the one."

"That crazy kid."

"So long, Saxon. I'll take my leave of Rita on the porch. And tell Rose I am sorry I will not hear her sing again, most likely."

"That's very . . . kind of you, Marshal."

Rita regarded Longarm nervously as he stepped out onto the veranda. "Did you see Dad?" she asked.

"Yes, I did," he replied, doffing his hat as he pulled up in front of her.

Rita's face was pale and drawn. It was obvious she knew all about her father's past and what that could mean to a federal marshal. Though no one in this valley knew who it was Longarm had come to find, there were many who knew they could be on Longarm's list.

"Well, Rita, this is goodbye. I got the man I came after—Mike Deaver. Right now, he's stashed away good and proper. I'll be catching the stage out of Snake Flat first thing in the morning. So thanks for everything."

The color flowed back into Rita's face. For an instant her eyes closed, as if she were uttering a silent prayer of thanksgiving.

"But, Marshal," she said, "it is we who should be thanking you."

"It's very nice of you to say that, Rita." He bent and kissed her lightly on the cheek. She blushed, then reached out, took his shoulders firmly, and kissed him on the lips. He felt the salt of her tears as he broke the kiss and stood back.

Putting his hat back on, he hurriedly descended the veranda steps and swung into his saddle. Lifting the black to a canter, he turned in his saddle to wave back to Rita and saw that Rose and Saxon had come out onto the veranda and joined her in waving goodbye.

The next afternoon, Longarm nudged the jehu a few miles south of Snake Flat, as the stagecoach started up a gentle grade.

"This is the spot," he said.

The jehu nodded and hauled back on the reins, then leaned his foot on the brake. The dust billowed up from the wheels, and their only other passenger, a whiskey drummer, stuck his head out the coach window.

"What are we stopping here for?" he demanded.

Longarm and the jehu climbed down. The jehu glanced in at the unhappy drummer.

"We got to go in the woods for a minute. Do you mind?"

"Oh. No, of course not."

As Longarm and the jehu moved into the brush, Longarm saw the whiskey drummer resume the sampling of his wares.

Mike Deaver was where Longarm had left him, close in under the boulder, buried up to his neck. But was he still alive? Longarm wondered, as he began to pull away the damp brush and the layers of pine needles. Deaver was still bound securely and the gag remained in his mouth. As Longarm hunkered down beside him, he saw Deaver's body move weakly. Then his eyes flickered open. Longarm felt some relief. Despite the awful stench, the man was alive.

It took a lot of punishment to kill some people.

Longarm got to his feet and stood back. "I suggest we dump him in the rear boot until we get to the next way station and clean him up. What do you think?"

"Well, I sure as hell ain't goin' to let him sit in my coach! Not with him smellin' like that!"

"Done. Now, if you'll just give me a hand."

The two men lugged the barely conscious Deaver to the coach, eased him not very gently into the boot, then closed the leather flap.

A moment later, as the driver gathered up the ribbons and set the stage in motion, he glanced over at Longarm. "That's some package you got there, Marshal. And you sure as hell came a long way to get it."

"I did at that," Longarm admitted, a slight, rueful smile breaking his countenance.

The rattle and roar of the stage precluded any further talk between them, and Longarm leaned back to watch the landscape flow by.

He was already rehearsing what he would tell Billy Vail. And it would be the truth—as far as it went. Jake Telford had been driven from the valley, but before he went he did not admit to Longarm that he was Babe Warner.

On the other hand, Longarm *was* bringing in Mike Deaver, one of the members of a gang which had eluded Wallace in Canada some years ago. Not only that, but Deaver was also guilty of killing two prospectors in Utah a year before, then raping a settler's wife not long afterward. The son of a bitch had even tried to kill a deputy U. S. marshal, and Longarm would experience no reluctance at all in testifying to that.

Longarm did not like playing this kind of game with Billy Vail. But, hell, Mike Deaver deserved a jail cell and the hangman's noose that might follow a hell of a lot more than did Dan Saxon. And some day, if he ever got around to telling the plain, unvarnished truth of it to Billy Vail over a few beers, Longarm had no doubt the old lawman would agree.

But only after a short argument, of course.

Watch for

LONGARM AND THE BLACKFOOT GUNS

seventy-seventh novel in the bold
LONGARM series from Jove

coming in May!

5

LONGARM

Explore the exciting Old West with
one of the men who made it wild!